Going Home

CLOVERTON ROMANCE BOOK ZERO

HAVEN SAUNDERS WITH MARCI WILSON

MAHANNA MEDIA, LLC

Chapter One

Since Dean Gorman hadn't been back to Cloverton in twelve years, going straight to the old mill as soon as he returned seemed fitting. Like many local teens back in the day, he had worked in the office until he turned eighteen and was legally allowed to be on the floor. However, unlike many of the locals, Dean had decided to move on to greener pastures. After two days of tasting sawdust, he packed his camera and left Cloverton in the rearview.

And he didn't look back.

Though Dean had regrets about how he left, he didn't regret leaving. What he left behind, though... He'd never gotten over that.

He didn't know the mill had closed until a year after the fact. That's when the nightmares began. For nearly a month straight, Dean dreamed of the mill. He dreamed of chaos, fires, and accidents, none of which had happened during his tenure there.

Still, the mill haunted him.

Which was why he had to come back.

Between assignments as a freelance photojournalist, Dean always had his own projects, and this one had been years in the making. He'd spent a summer documenting behind the scenes of county fairs across the country, slept on the ground for weeks while highlighting the experiences of an unhoused person, and had hiked through the Alaskan wilderness with Innuit women searching for a missing daughter.

In the back of his mind, though, he'd always wanted to return to Cloverton and see what had happened to the mill, and consequently the town. He'd seen this scenario a hundred times in his travels. Knowing Cloverton had succumbed to a similar fate made his heart ache. He needed a way to process what had happened to his hometown. That's how the *Defunct Americans* project began. Dean had been traveling the country on his motorcycle shooting shuttered factories and dilapidated towns to highlight the growing invisibility of blue-collar America.

Through his explorations, he'd made many friends, taken thousands of photographs, and now, it was time for the capstone of it all.

Cloverton Lumber.

Dean pulled into the oversize vacant parking lot as dusk settled on a balmy July evening. The building looked more hulking than ever. Sprawling and gray.

He got off his bike and wiped his face with his T-shirt. It'd been a while since he had been in Illinois in the summer. For some reason, the Midwest heat always felt brutal.

Putting a hand to his forehead to block some of the direct sunlight, he stared off into the distance. If he had continued along the road, he would have ended up right in the heart of town. Main Street. He couldn't help but wonder, was the square still the same? Were the stores still open?

He'd driven past the Schnyder's hotel on his way in. It looked even more rundown than it had when he'd left town.

It would break his heart if Cloverton was suffering like so many of the other towns he'd traipsed through over the past month and a half.

For that reason, he decided he wouldn't be making any visits to old haunts or old friends.

Even if there were people he had wondered about.

His parents had retired to Arizona after the mill closed. They had no reason to stick around. Which meant Dean had no reason to visit. None that he would admit to anyway.

He had ignored the genesis of social media almost to a fault. Once a month he sent photos to his assistant who managed to do whatever she needed to do to keep his brand doing whatever it was people did online.

But staying off social media was, what he believed, a testament to his work. It kept it fresh, grounded, nostalgic even.

He had a simple website that he let his agent run. And that was good enough for him.

The tradeoff, though, was not knowing where the people he cared about had ended up all these years since he left. He missed them. He missed the connections from his childhood. But he wasn't sure he was ready to face the past that had broken his heart.

"Three days. That's all," he muttered to himself, retrieving his rucksack from the back of his bike.

Three days to explore the grounds, get all the photos he needed, and then be out of there. He'd have to find a place in one of the buildings to hide the bike to avoid any suspicion from local police.

Before going inside, Dean snapped a quick photo of Cloverton bathed in swaths of orange sunset. That would be a good one to have to show the symbolism of the end of what was.

Dean knew the mill like the back of his hand, and, consequently, knew how to get inside with the least amount of effort or risk of being seen. He ignored all the caution tape and the signs that suggested he'd be prosecuted for trespassing and made his way to the administrative entrance at the top of a white metal staircase that looked so rusty one would think the mill had been closed for ten years instead of five.

He could have contacted the city and gotten a permit. Perhaps even gotten a tour. But the fewer people who knew he was in town, the better.

With a little tinkering of the lock and a few forceful pushes of his shoulder, Dean gained access to the mill.

It was deathly quiet inside. Every step he took echoed through the wide halls.

According to the research he'd done, all the equipment had been sold. All that was left were the offices and gangways above the sawmill floor.

Orange light streamed through the open ceiling, casting a glow over graffiti and debris probably left by local teens and transients. The sight made Dean smile. The abandoned building was like all the others he'd highlighted.

"Now to make camp," he said to himself.

Officer Melanie Hart lowered her head at the sound of approaching footsteps. Determined to stay out of the line of fire, she focused on the paperwork she was filling out on her computer as Chief Wilkes neared her desk.

"Hudson!"

Fellow police officer Chet Hudson looked up from his desk which was adjacent to Mel's.

"I want you to take a walk around the mill when you get a few. Someone reported movement out there."

The caution tape and warning signs were a laughable attempt at staving off local riffraff. The main door had a combination lock box that held the keys. Every police officer and rescue worker had the code, and a few of the riffraff had probably figured it out as well.

What the mill really needed was ongoing surveillance but no one, not even the city, was willing to put money into that effort. If Mel was in charge, she'd pay to have it bulldozed before someone got hurt out there. The temptation of a big empty warehouse was too much to resist for a lot of the youth in town. Exploring the old mill was practically a rite of passage for area teens.

"Someone said there was a guy on a motorcycle outside."

Mel stopped typing. For some reason, the hair on the back of her neck stood on end. "What kind of motorcycle?"

"I don't know. They didn't get a close look."

Mel swallowed and shook her head. *Plenty of people own motorcycles.*

"Give it a once over, would you?"

Chet nodded. "Sure thing."

"Great. Hart," Wilkes said as she walked away with a nod toward Mel.

Mel smiled at the chief before returning to her work. Out of the corner of her eye, she spotted Chet about to open his mouth to talk to her. "Don't even think about asking. I've got paperwork to catch up on."

Chet collapsed back in his chair. "How do you do that?"

"Got two kids. That'll give you a third eye fast."

Chet chuckled. "One doesn't count for anything?"

"Oh, hell no. You need two of them to cause real mischief."

"Erik causes plenty of mischief on his own."

Mel laughed. "Erik is the sweetest kid, and you know it."

"That's why you always gotta be on your toes. You never know when he's gonna turn on you." They both laughed for a moment before Chet picked up where he left off.

"Come on, Mel. I hate that place. It creeps me out. I need backup."

"And I need to do my paperwork."

"Sure you do."

Mel glared at him. It was a fond sort of glare. Chet and Mel had been partners on cases and beats more times than she could count. They were fast friends from the moment Mel joined the force. That was a bonus in a coworker because he didn't tell on her when she waited until the last minute to do paperwork.

She minimized the form she was filling out and started reading the webpage before her. She'd been on the *Net Stars Soccer Camp* site nearly twenty times, intending to enroll her two girls, Hannah and Ellie, before school had even ended. However, every time she did, she couldn't stop staring at the price tag.

The camp had already given her a deal since she was enrolling two children instead of one, but that barely skimmed the surface of the money Mel would have to pull together for soccer camp.

Next, she pulled up a spreadsheet titled *July Budget* and started scrolling through.

What else can I cut back on?

Every month was like this. She couldn't skimp on groceries or gas or the mortgage or utilities. That didn't leave much to play around with when she had two mouths to feed, not including hers.

Fucking Mark.

Mel had that thought at least three times a day for the last five years. Sometimes while doing something as simple as brushing her teeth. Other times while pulling her credit card out at the grocery store. And sometimes, she cursed her ex-husband simply for fun.

Mark had skipped town soon after the mill closed. He lost his job, and his marbles went with it. They'd gotten married right out of high school with Ellie already on the way and, while it wasn't a perfect marriage, Mel had thought it was serviceable. Survivable.

Mark, on the other hand, decided to cut and run to go *find* himself.

She had been heartbroken at first. Now she was pissed off.

But in moments like this, where she was desperate to scrape together the money to register her girls into soccer camp, it hurt. Mel had long been over Mark leaving her, but she still didn't understand how he could leave his children without so much as a goodbye.

Mel hadn't heard from him again except through divorce papers, which she signed gratefully. It didn't surprise her that he never paid the court-ordered child support. She'd taken him to court once, but she wasn't ready to go through that again.

She was strong. She could do this.

"I'll buy you coffee," Chet interrupted her silence. "And a pastry," Chet added when she didn't respond. "I know you can't resist a scone."

Damn it. He was right. And in the heat of summer, the office became a humid mess and started to smell like a high school locker room. She could go for an iced latte about now. "Fine. I'll go."

Chet jumped to his feet with a grin. "That's the spirit."
"But I'm only going for the coffee."
"I know. You won't regret it."
Mel scoffed. She wasn't sure about that.

Chapter Two

Dean liked camping as a kid. The skills his dad had taught him made life on the road much easier to navigate. If he couldn't find a hotel, he could pitch a tent wherever he pleased.

After parking his bike and setting up camp, he started walking around Cloverton Logging, snapping photos of broken windows and dusty corners. Everything in the world had a tragic amount of beauty to Dean. The mill was no different. It was harder to look at, though.

Dean had crafted his life away from his hometown for a reason. This place felt like a dead end. Now, at twenty-eight years old, he was starting to realize that he'd pushed everything about Cloverton so far away he was starting to miss it.

As he explored the interior of the building, Dean spotted a mouse skittering across the floor. He stopped in his tracks and smiled. He took a few quiet steps forward, following the path of the mouse, making sure his shoes weren't too loud against the floor.

Creeping closer and closer to a pile of wood scraps, Dean spotted the mouse again, jumping around as if the wood was a jungle gym. He crouched down, aiming his camera.

The rodent stopped for him as if knowing its picture was being taken. Dean zoomed in so close, he could make out the whiskers. A factory mouse. When he'd worked in the office, they were always finding droppings in the break room.

He had been the only one not scared of the mice and was adamant about catching them humanely to release in the fields. Without warning, the mouse leaped and disappeared into the wood scraps.

"Damn it," Dean grunted, letting his arm fall onto his knee.

Animals were always more aware of their surroundings than humans, and the disappearing mouse was a harbinger of what was to come. Moments later, Dean heard the slamming of a car door.

He stood and looked toward the entrance to the warehouse, a roll-up sheet door that had held together despite the rest of the mill's disrepair.

Several bangs echoed through the empty building causing Dean to jump.

Someone was trying to get in.

He needed to hide fast. As quietly as he could, he bounded up the metal staircase that led to the foreman's office. That had been the perfect place to take cover the night before. And now, to hide.

He slipped into the foreman's office, leaving the door propped open as he had found it. Moments later the sound of the metal door rolling up filled the space. Whoever it was, didn't seem to be concerned about being caught.

"This place gives me the creeps," a voice announced. A voice that sent familiar shivers down his spine.

No…

"Relax, we're not walking into a horror movie."

"Says you. Cops are always the first victims."

"No, Black people are," the man said. "Cute little blondes like you tend to get away."

The woman laughed. Dean knew that laugh.

"Okay," she said. "That's fair."

Dean needed to know if his mind was playing tricks on him. He peeked out from behind the door to see if he could spot the source of the voice.

The past came flooding back the second he saw her.

Mel Callaghan. *Hart.* She had gotten married to that jackass, Mark.

Dean would have recognized her anywhere. Even though her silky blonde hair was shorter now and she donned a uniform instead of his oversize sweatshirt and what had been her signature tight jeans, it was definitely the woman he'd fallen so hard for in high school.

As beautiful as he remembered.

Accompanying her was a tall Black man. Their police uniforms must have been hellishly hot on a July day. The two of them clearly had a rapport, a history.

Dean had a history with Mel, too. One that he'd still hadn't gotten over.

"I don't know, Chet, seems fine," Mel said as her flashlight illuminated a corner of the warehouse.

"Just a quick walk around."

"Whoever's been here is gone by now."

Dean was glad he'd ditched his motorcycle in one of the smaller buildings, one that didn't seem to draw as much attention.

Mel glanced around the building. Though he couldn't see her blue eyes, he remembered them vividly.

"Five minutes, Mel."

Mel. Who was this guy to be calling her Mel? Dean recognized the other cop. Remembered him as a young rookie when Dean and his friends used to get bored and cause mischief. Now he was calling her Mel?

Dean didn't like that. Not one bit.

She scanned the area. "Sorry. This place reminds me of Mark."

Chet sighed, continuing his search. "I know it does. You can take a look outside."

"I'm fine."

She wasn't. Ten years may have gone by since he'd seen her, but he remembered all her tells.

After all, they'd been childhood best friends. And by the end, he'd been in love with her.

That unrequited love had been the catalyst for his decision to leave. For ten years, Dean had carried the shame that he hadn't had the guts to tell her. He pretended he'd left Cloverton in a blaze of glory, but really, he moped out with his tail between his legs, knowing the girl he loved was about to marry someone else.

And that someone else had turned out to be a jackass.

"Erik is doing Net Stars, right?" Mel asked out of the blue, shining her light in a different corner now.

"Yeah. Did you sign the girls up?"

Mel sighed. "I plan to but it's so expensive."

Chet stopped and watched Mel for a moment as she peered at the pile of wood Dean had been photograph- ing earlier. "You need some help with the fee?"

"Don't even mention that, Chet."

"I'm only saying that—"

"I'm simply shooting the shit, Hudson," Mel said. "I wasn't asking for a loan."

This was breaking Dean's heart. Sure, he didn't have social media. But his mother was always willing to up- date him on the goings on in Cloverton. She'd told him that Mel had two beautiful girls made exactly in her image, thank God, since her ex looked like an ogre. She was no longer married. The details, he wasn't sure of. All he knew was that she was a single mom.

Strong, obstinate, and determined. That was Mel. She wouldn't take a handout if she could help it.

"I'll have the money together by the due date. I can pick up a few extra shifts and leave the girls with my mom and—" Mel cut herself off with a terrified scream that rattled the warehouse's bones.

"What? What is it?" Chet shouted, rushing over to her.

"A mouse! I saw a mouse!"

Chet threw his hands up and let out a frustrated moan. "You're kidding. You screamed like that because of a mouse?"

Mel shook with disgust. "It was big, Chet. I wasn't expecting to see mice."

"It's an abandoned building. What *did* you expect?"

"I don't know! A transient. A serial killer. Dead bodies. But not a *mouse*."

Chet's frustration turned into laughter, and Mel followed slowly after that.

Dean found himself smiling endearingly as he looked down from his perch. He might not like how familiar Chet, was with her, but he liked that the man could make her laugh.

"Come on," Chet said, "let's get out of here. You're right. Whoever was here is long gone."

"I need that coffee."

"Yeah, yeah. You're lucky you're funny."

"Actually, I think *you're* lucky I'm funny," Mel teased, and then started rushing off in the direction of the rolling door.

Chet followed behind her but stopped at the door. His gaze shot to the balcony where Dean was hidden. Dean froze. He dared not breathe. Thankfully, Chet stared up for only a few moments before he walked the rest of the way out.

Dean listened to the roll-top door scrape downward, the loud clamping of a metal chain, and then the rumble of a car.

Finally, silence.

Though the world around him was quiet, Dean's mind was filled with memories of laughter, long talks, and a lifetime of hearing her voice. All the bittersweet nostalgia of his youth that he'd pushed down and tried to keep quiet all these years was suddenly rustling to life.

He'd been firm with himself. No visits. No old haunts.

No reason to bring back the past, Dean reminded himself.

Though secretly, he knew the only reason he was avoiding seeing Melanie Hart was a cowardice he would never name.

Chapter Three

Mel didn't usually work Saturday nights, but she'd requested extra shifts to earn a little overtime. So there she was, exhausted and not really in the mood to patrol the town. Not that she had any other plans for the weekend.

"No," Mel stated firmly, "no sleepover tonight."

"*Mom*," her eldest daughter whined through the phone.

Mel was used to this song and dance. Ellie was approaching double-digits in age. Fourth grade had inspired quite a bit of rebellion and, consequently, she was always trying to get under Mel's skin.

"Sorry, but we didn't plan for this. You have to plan ahead. You know this, Ellie." Mel pushed open the door to The Coffee Nut.

Ryan Carter gave her a nod from behind the counter. He knew her order without her asking and set to making her drink.

There were times when Mel wondered what life might be like beyond her hometown. But moments like these always reminded her how grateful she was to be somewhere where she was known.

When Ellie began to whine again, Mel cut her off. "Sorry, there's no winning this argument. You're staying home and that's that."

"Fine," her daughter said angrily.

"I love you. Bye." Mel ended the call before she could get another earful of Ellie's complaints. "Sorry about that, Ryan."

"No worries at all."

Sure, she needed to be saving money, but she also couldn't afford to fall asleep on night patrol.

"Be on alert tonight," Ryan said, coming to the counter with her iced latte. "There's a storm headed our way, fast."

Mel glanced out the front window of The Coffee Nut. The evening sky looked clear. No storm in sight. "Huh. I haven't heard about that."

"Meteorology isn't *really* a science. It's all guessing, isn't it?"

"Well, for my sake, let's hope they got it wrong this time." Mel pulled out her wallet.

Ryan waved his hands. "On the house tonight, Officer Hart."

"Oh, come on, Ryan. Don't be a saint."

"I'll be a saint if I like. Now take your coffee before I change my mind."

Mel smiled sweetly and didn't press any harder. She'd take any win she could get. "Fine. But here." She put a few dollars in the tip jar. "At the very least."

Ryan gave her a nod. "Be safe out there."

"Thanks." Mel sipped the latte. "Mmm. Delicious."

She started to make her way back out of the shop, taking note of a conversation happening at a table near the front. "I think we should stay in tonight," the woman murmured, looking at her phone. "This storm front is moving in fast."

Yeesh. Mel hadn't heard a word about a storm, yet it seemed to be the talk of the town. Once again, she hoped any bad weather would hold off, at least until her night patrol was over. Either that, or Cloverton would be uneventful this Saturday night and she could hunker down in her car and wait for the rain to pass.

Barely an hour later, Mel was cruising toward one of the subdivisions outside of town when she heard the rolling thunder in the distance.

In the dark, she couldn't track how the clouds were moving until a crack of lightning burst across the horizon. And they were coming in like stampeding rhinos.

The storm was closing in fast, like Ryan had predicted.

Which was, of course, when her com went off.

"Hart, we had a call that someone is seeing some activity at the old mill again. Can you go check it out?"

Mel's heart bottomed out. God, she hated that place. "What kind of activity?"

"Some lights," the dispatcher sighed. "Pretty sure it's reflections from the lightning."

Mel gripped the steering wheel harder. Why couldn't it have been anywhere else? Any*thing* else? In a small town like Cloverton, major police activity was rare, but she would rather have to tackle a man streaking through town than have to check out the old mill.

"Copy that," she said and headed toward the mill, toward the storm.

The backroads of Cloverton were dark with only a few streetlights at intersections. Which is what made the mill so ominous. Before it closed, the parking lot would be bathed in fluorescent white after dark. Now it was a black void on the horizon.

Except...

Mel swore she saw some light from the administration windows.

"Damn it," she muttered. She'd hoped she could poke her head in and call it done, but now she'd have to actually do a thorough search.

By the time she arrived in the gravel parking lot, rain started pelting the car. If this was the beginning of the storm, Mel didn't want to be on the road in the middle of it. Maybe this was a blessing in disguise.

She climbed out of her car and trotted to the main roll-top door.

Mel tapped the code into the digital lock and waited for the beep to indicate she'd correctly released the latch. The rain made gripping the metal a challenge, but after several attempts, she got the chain undone and yanked it off the door.

You got this.

She heaved the door up, hating how the sound bounced around her. There was no way to discreetly enter this building. If someone was there, they knew they'd been busted before the police ever entered. She pulled her flashlight off her belt and touched her gun in the process. Being a woman alone in the middle of nowhere, police officer or not, made her grateful she had a weapon.

The high beam of her flashlight glanced off the remains of the mill. Mel glanced back at the roll-top door and decided to leave it open so she could make a quick escape if necessary.

As she scanned her surroundings, the rain beat harder outside.

It wasn't loud enough, though, to obscure the sound of thumping metal.

Mel's stomach flipped and she jerked her flashlight in the direction of the sound. "Hello?"

Silence. Rain.

"Cloverton PD. Raise your hands and step out where I can see you."

Nothing.

Another sound made Mel jolt. She held her gun straight out, flashlight over her wrist, going closer to the sound. "If you show yourself, we can make this easy. No one has to get hurt."

As she scanned her flashlight across the empty mill, the beam glinted off something. A mirror? Glass? She refocused her light in the direction of the flash.

On the ground sat...a camera?

Mel slowly moved closer as if it might be a bomb. What the hell was a camera doing on the factory floor?

There was another sound, this time from behind her.

Now, she was pissed.

Mel started to walk with purpose in the direction of the sound, then stopped in her tracks when her beam landed on a familiar face.

No. It couldn't be.

Though his hair was longer, and a thin layer of facial hair covered the lower part of his face, she knew who it was instantly.

For a split second, she thought she had seen a ghost.

But... It couldn't be him.

The man held up his hands in surrender. "Hey, Mel."

She shook her head. She had wished for him to come back so many times but had given up on the hope he'd return.

"That's my camera over there."

Mel extended her arm when he took a step in her direction. "Do not move."

"Okay, easy."

"Do you have a weapon on you?" she asked.

"Are you kidding?"

"No. Turn out your pockets."

He followed her instructions, producing a wallet, some keys, and what looked like an SD card.

Thunder rattled the frame of the building. "Drop it."

He put the stuff on the ground in front of him.

"Back away ten steps."

Hands still in surrender, the man moved away. His gray eyes never wavered from her intense gaze.

Mel closed the gap between herself and the wallet, keeping her focus on the man until she picked it up to check the ID.

Sure enough. Dean Gorman. Still with the same photo from his driver's license all those years ago. In the photo, he had a mop of golden-brown hair on his head and was smiling like the dork he used to be. He didn't look like a dork now. His hair was short, and his facial hair trimmed.

Mel raised the beam of her flashlight back to the man as she holstered her gun. He looked older and wiser...sexier. "Hi, Dean."

His smile returned. "I was worried that—" He started to walk toward her.

Mel stepped back and moved her hand back to the hip where her weapon rested. "Don't come near me."

He stopped dead in his tracks, eyes wide.

Mel had wanted this reunion for years. She always thought that the moment she saw Dean again, she'd run to him, wrap him in her arms, and never let go.

But in reality, all she felt was anger.

She not only wanted answers. She *deserved* them. "What the hell are you doing here, and why has it taken you so long to come back?"

Chapter Four

Being on the other end of Mel's gun was not the way Dean ever imagined them reuniting. He was grateful it was tucked back into her holster. However, even with her gun put away, the laser stare he was getting from her ice-blue eyes was brutal.

"I'm waiting," she said coolly. "*Dean.*"

"Sorry, sorry, you're just so...intimidating."

The corner of her lip turned up in a smirk that only lasted for a second. "Talk."

"I'm working on a project."

She raised an eyebrow. "A project?"

The blaring flashlight was starting to make his head hurt. "Do you mind not pointing that thing right at me anymore?"

Mel shut off the flashlight and tucked it away. "You're doing a project here?"

Instead of the severe white light bouncing back on Mel, she was bathed in the dim lights from the parking lot, save a bright crack of lightning every now and then. "A photo series."

Her eyes started to narrow.

"I'm traveling around the country going to abandoned buildings to show how things have changed and how blue-collar America is—"

"So you came here to use us."

This was why he wanted to leave well enough alone. "Not to use you. The town. I'm going to take photos of the mill."

"The town *is* the mill. It may have closed, but that doesn't mean it isn't still a part of who we are."

Dean gulped. He could feel the intense anger boiling under Mel's skin. "Sure. I get it. That's part of why I want the photos."

"Your parents moved away a few years ago. Where have you been staying?"

Shit. "Here."

"Squatting."

"Well—"

"You're trespassing. I could arrest you."

Their standoff continued as they stared each other down in the amber streetlights streaming into the building. So many memories. So much left unsaid. And this is how she wanted to start things off?

"You're joking, right."

"Nope. It's my job."

"Come on, Mel."

"Don't 'come on, Mel,' me, *Dean*."

He didn't think he deserved the way she said his name with such vitriol and disdain. All he'd done was follow his own path. Like she'd followed hers. Wasn't that fair? "Fine. Please don't arrest me."

"You have a lot of nerve coming back here to make money off this place."

"That's not what this is."

"It's not? You're here to take pictures for old time's sake?"

He wanted to relax. Wanted her to relax, too. Maybe then her anger would abate, and they could talk. Reconnect. It seemed serendipitous the way they reunited. He'd avoided her the day before when she walked back into his life. Now the universe was giving him a second chance.

But she wasn't going to make it easy.

"It's my personal project. I'm not on an assignment for someone else. This is a story I want to tell."

Mel considered him through the darkness. "Still sounds selfish."

Dean threw his hands up and let them land against his thighs with a slap. "Maybe."

It was clear that Mel had determined how she felt about him, and he wasn't going to change that feeling by saying anything else.

"Be gone by tomorrow morning or else." Her voice cut through the pounding of rain on the windows. Then, she turned on her heels and started for the open roll-top door.

Dean wasn't going to let her walk away like that. Not after all this time. "Mel, wait."

She continued walking.

He picked up the contents of his pockets from the floor and stuffed them back in his jeans before going after her. "You can't go out there. It's pouring rain."

"Obviously."

She had always been bullheaded. When she set her sights on something, she went for it. Right now, she was set on returning to her car.

"It's been ten years. Can we at least talk? Catch up?"

"I'm on duty, Dean." She looked over her shoulder at him as if he was a speck of dust. "Besides, I don't hang out with criminals."

There was a time when they were running around Cloverton, ready to wreak harmless havoc, with cops on their tails all the time. They weren't necessarily bad kids, but they certainly had been bored in this tiny town.

"Don't go out there in this storm." Dean gently grabbed her by the arm to stop her.

She turned swiftly, shaking his hand off. Though only five foot two, Mel carried herself like a giant. "Don't tell me what to do."

There she was. Same old Mel.

She walked out into the storm toward the police cruiser as if nothing was happening.

Dean pointed to the gravel bridge spanning the ditch that separated the mill from the frontage road. "You won't make it over the ditch. The gravel always gets too loose."

"I'll be fine!"

"Mel, stick it out a little while longer! We don't have to talk, but I want you to be safe."

"I have a hard time believing you want anything for me Dean. When was the last time you paid me a passing thought?" she shot back at top volume to be heard over the rain, wind, and thunder.

Dean stopped, feet squelching in the muddy parking lot, and stared at her. If only she had known how not a day had gone past that he had not thought about her. Even if it was a quiet thought. A memory, a wondering, a well wish.

And from her anger, it was clear to him she hadn't stopped thinking about him either.

A siren began to blare through the air. Not a police siren, but one like a shrill crying whale. The tornado siren.

The night sky was too dark to see where a tornado might be forming. It would be ridiculous to assume they weren't in harm's way. Dean stared at Mel, waiting for her gaze to return to him, and when it did, he raised his eyebrows. "Will you come back inside *now*?"

He breathed a sigh of relief as she marched past him back into the mill. He followed behind her.

"Help me close this," she yelled over the sounds of the weather.

They pulled the roll top down, leaving them encased in the old mill. Just the two of them.

Dean glanced at Mel. Her arms were pressed over her chest as she started to shiver. Her body was drenched from head to toe causing her blonde hair to cling to her head.

"Come on. We should go wait this out in the bath-room," he suggested, pointing to a doorway off the main floor.

She sighed. "Lead the way."

As they made their way through the mill, the rain started to abate. That wasn't a good sign. Rain usually stopped before a tornado. Dean could recall one time that he was eating dinner at the Callaghan house when the power went out mid-storm. Then the warning went off, and they all had to pile into the basement with their bowls of mac and cheese. The warning went on for what felt like hours.

Good times.

This time, though, it was Dean and Mel and they weren't eight, but twenty-eight. And they'd both lived a lot more life.

They went into the men's restroom, marked by a plastic sign with a figure with two lopped-off legs. Inside, all that remained was the tile and a few shattered mirrors that had been spraypainted over with the words: *We'll all die here.*

"Timely," she muttered to herself, staring at the graffiti. "Did you do this?"

He glanced at her and half-smiled. "Nah. Been years since I've done something like that."

"Mmm. Shocking." With a frown, she clicked the mic attached to her shoulder and radioed in her location, advising the dispatcher she'd be riding out the siren at the mill. Once the dispatcher confirmed, Mel turned down the radio so the crackling voice wouldn't be quite so loud.

She leaned against the opposite wall and rolled her face toward the ceiling, making it abundantly clear that this was going to be a long night.

Lucky for Dean, he'd grown to be a patient man.

Chapter Five

Ten minutes of listening to the muted tornado siren left Mel feeling antsy.

Though she considered herself a strong person, waiting was not her strong suit. Labor with her first daughter took nearly twenty-four hours. She didn't complain about the pain once, but she had grown weary of the waiting.

Unfortunately for her, Dean knew this about her. He knew everything about her and yet, after so much time apart, he felt like a stranger. Mel didn't recognize him the way she used to.

She was now sitting on the tile floor, having cleared the space with her shoe. Dean, on the other hand, was pacing. Each lap he took, Mel's irritation mounted. If he stood still, she could pretend he wasn't there, but she couldn't ignore the way he was constantly crunching the debris under his shoes as he walked by.

Eventually, Dean stopped his pattern of back and forth and pulled a pack of gum from his pocket.

Mel's cheek ticked with aggravation.

"Want one?"

She shook her head.

Dean put the gum stick in his mouth and then ran his hand through his wet hair.

Silence returned to the bathroom. As silent as it could be with a tornado siren blaring in the background, wind roaring, and rain pelting against the roof.

"So," he said, "how have you been?"

"We don't have to do this."

"I'm trying to make conversation. Who knows how long we'll be cooped up in here."

Mel rested her head on the wall, closing her eyes. He had a point.

And at least it might pass the time a bit better than waiting in silence. "I've been good."

He chuckled and leaned against a sink that was already half broken off the wall. He seemed to test how sturdy the structure was before crossing his ankles and resting his palms on the dirty surface behind him. "You want to elaborate?"

She blinked, trying to pull the reins back on feelings she thought were extinct in her body. Turned out they'd been dormant. "I have a rewarding job. It's hard sometimes, but it's worth the bad days. I have two great kids. So... I've been good."

He nodded. "That's good to hear."

Mel returned to staring at the floor. That was enough conversation, in her opinion.

"Mom told me that Mark left after the mill closed."

"Yup. He left me and our kids like we meant nothing to him."

Dean was silent.

She smiled to herself. As far as she was concerned, having him speechless was a win. "Is that what you wanted to hear?"

"Not what I *wanted* to hear but—"

"He needed to go find himself," she said bitterly, "because all he'd ever been was a mill worker and my husband and a father. There had to be more in this world than that, right? So he left, and I haven't heard from him since."

Dean frowned. "That's a lot."

"Yeah, a bit of an understatement."

He chewed his gum for a few moments. "I'm sorry."

"Are you fucking serious right now?"

"Good to know you haven't lost that mouth of yours, even after motherhood," he murmured.

"You're sorry? I tell you about my marriage ending and single motherhood and you're sorry. Wait until I tell you about how my best friend disappeared without a word right before my wedding."

Dean rubbed his chin. "Look, this isn't easy for me either, Mel."

"Oh, I guess I should have sugar-coated my life for you."

"Damn, you've got an attitude."

She let out a scoff. "I've earned it."

"I never said you didn't."

Mel shook her head. "You been gallivanting around for ten years, nowhere to be seen, but I am still in Cloverton. I never left. You had no excuse not to stay in touch with me. But did you? Did you ever call or email or send me a text? No. Not once."

Dean tried to interrupt, but she steamrolled right over him.

"Everyone here is so proud of you. Hometown boy done good. Our little shining star. We see every picture you've sold to the fancy magazines and how your work is gracing the walls of national park welcome centers. Hell, I couldn't watch cable news during the last election without seeing your credit on half the photos of the campaign trails."

Dean had a stupid smile on his face she wished she could slap off. "So you've seen my work, then?"

"I can't escape it. I might have been pissed off you left, but I'm proud of you and your work. I always knew you were talented and that you could do awesome things, and I..." Mel went silent and shook her head, not willing to say what she was thinking.

"You what?" he pushed.

She hated that tears stung her eyes but was happy that he probably couldn't see them in the near-dark room. "I bet you don't even know what my daughters' names are."

"Hannah and Ellie," he said quietly. "I'm up to date on all things Mel Callaghan. I mean, *Hart*."

She stared at him. Unwilling to give him credit for his correct answer.

"Mel Hart," he repeated as if it tasted bad. "I know I've been a shit friend. I mean, the way we left things..." Dean scratched the back of his head. "I have regrets."

"I find that hard to believe."

He laughed sadly. "I'm sure you do."

She let her gaze linger on his.

"I regret leaving the way I did. I should have been supportive. I should have...been at your wedding."

Mel had stuffed that wound deep inside her without it ever having healed. "Well, it's fine. It didn't work out, so you didn't miss anything."

"Don't talk about it like that. I know you loved him."

Her stomach dropped. The truth was, she hadn't loved him. She grew to love him as the father of their children, but that's not why she'd married him.

She'd married him because she got pregnant, and marriage felt like the only thing that made sense. Not that she'd ever dared to say that aloud.

"I've seen the pictures of you and your girls. They look like you. And I can tell they're as spunky."

Mel laughed despite herself. "That's a nice way of putting it. *Spunky.*"

"It's what you are. It's why you were my best friend. We were both a little... free-spirited."

"We were punks," she said.

He laughed. "We tried, but at the end of the day we were posers."

"Yeah. Well, at least I was. You're out there living that life we always said we'd live. I'm...I'm doing exactly what we said we *weren't* going to do. I'm trapped in this shit town with no way out."

He looked down at the tips of his boots. "I wish I hadn't missed out on so much."

"That's life."

"It didn't have to be." He took a step toward her.

Her heart started to pound in her chest. He eased to the ground across from her, crossing his legs.

"I'm really proud of you," he said.

She snorted.

He chuckled softly. "You're still doing that self-deprecating thing, huh?"

"Can't help it."

He stared at her hands for several seconds before reaching out and taking one, squeezing it gently. His touch was familiar and comforting. Even after all this time. And that was more terrifying than any horror movie Mel could dream up. She pulled her hand free from his, wiping the heat of his touch along her slacks.

"I mean it. I'm proud of you."

Silence unfolded around them. True silence now. The siren had gone quiet.

"Oh shit," Mel muttered. "The siren stopped." She pushed herself up. "I should go. They might need me out there."

Before he could stop her, she brushed by him and left the safety of the old, broken-down men's room.

Chapter Six

Dean accompanied Mel to the entrance of the mill where they stood and watched the rain begin to pour again. He pointed at the distance. The amber light above the entrance to the parking lot shone on a grim sight. The causeway between the parking lot and the road had washed out leaving it impassable in the current state.

"You'll have to wait it out," Dean said definitively.

She sighed. "Damn it." Mel spoke into the receiver on her shoulder, letting the station know she was stuck.

He was surprised she didn't fight him harder on it, but he wasn't going to question it. He would be grateful for any cooperation she gave him. Given the small size of Cloverton's emergency department, she would be stuck for some time. And Dean didn't mind that one bit.

She pulled a cell phone from the pocket at her thigh and tapped the screen a few times before putting it to her ear. "Hey, you guys okay?" She listened, nodded, and then looked up at the sky. "Well, stay put. I'm at the mill. The road washed out so I'm going to be here a while. Call Chet if you need anything." She ended the call and sighed.

"All's well?" he asked.

"Seems to be." She scanned the large room behind them. "So where the hell have you been sleeping?" Mel asked.

"Come on. I'll show you."

He led her up the metal staircase to the foreman's office. Dean had a way of really making himself at home in his campsites, and this one was no different.

"Jeez, you've got...everything."

As much of "everything" as a person could have on a motorcycle—which he hoped was safe in the other building. A small camp stove, a sleeping bag, a collapsible lantern, and many other necessities. "Well, you know, be prepared."

She laughed, loud and bawdy, and that gave Dean a little boost of confidence that they could rekindle their friendship. They were always laughing when they were younger. Nobody could amuse him like Mel.

"Let's get you out of those wet clothes, huh?"

Her eyes widened. "And into what?"

He went to his duffle. "I've got some shirts and sweatpants you can wear. You know, like in the old days."

She had worn his clothing plenty of times. An intimate act that had never felt that way. Now it felt intimate and purposeful as he handed over a set of clothes to her.

She looked around. "Where can I change?"

He walked toward a door in the corner and opened it for her. "Here. The foreman had a private bathroom. You can use that."

Mel smiled at him as she passed. "Thanks."

As soon as the door was shut, Dean put a hand against his sternum. *Easy... Steady...* This was all so much, so fast. He'd started the night trying to get some final photos. The storm dark was lending a specific quality to the mill that he wanted to explore.

Then, Mel showed up. Out of the blue. Ruined his shoot, nearly arrested him, sat with him through a tornado warning, and now, with the causeway washed out, she was...with him.

And it felt nice.

"You hungry?" Dean called out.

"Sure."

He rifled through his bag for the last few cans of food he had stowed away—beans and corn, canned chicken, and roasted peppers. He'd either have to make a grocery run in the morning or move on.

The door swung open, and Mel emerged with Dean's clothes swimming around her. She ran her hands through her wet hair and laughed. "It's a little big, but it'll do."

He half-smiled. "Yeah. It's okay?"

She nodded and started draping her clothes over the old desk so they could dry. "Better than my wet uniform for sure."

Dean started to pop open the cans. She peered at what he was making and grimaced.

"Oh, come on, it's not so bad."

"Sounds terrible."

Dean lit the stove and pulled out a collapsible pan. "Well, it's not. Besides, I have a recipe."

"A recipe? For camp food?"

"Have you still never been camping?"

She didn't answer before turning away. When Dean had gone camping with his dad and guy friends growing up, Mel had to be left at home, as were the rules.

"If this is your first camping experience, we're going to make it count."

Dean poured the cans into the pan. Once the contents started to boil, he produced a few baggies of seasoning and started to sprinkle them over the medley.

"Wow, you really come prepared."

"Have to. I might not have my own place, but I like to have my creature comforts."

"You don't have a house? An apartment?"

Dean shook his head. "No. Don't need one. I'm always traveling anyway."

"But you only have a bike. Don't you need places to store things?"

"I have a storage unit back in California."

"California," she repeated. "I've never been to California. In fact, I've never been west of Omaha."

Dean grabbed the sleeping bag and pulled it in front of the stove. "Sit."

Mel eased down. "I can't believe you do this all the time."

"Well, not all the time. Usually, a couple of months here and there when I'm not on assignment."

"On assignment."

"I know it's—" he interrupted anticipating her to jab him.

"Cool."

He stopped. He hadn't expected an actual compliment from her. "Right."

Neither of them spoke for a bit, sinking into the sounds of simmering food and the rain pattering on the roof and the window of the foreman's office that was miraculously still intact.

"How'd you get in here?" Mel asked softly.

"Can't reveal all my secrets."

She smiled. "I'm not going to arrest you, Dean."

"Oh yeah? How can I be so sure?" He grinned and wandered back to his bag, retrieving a fifth of whiskey. "Wouldn't be the first time you tricked me into something."

Mel hummed to herself. "I'm not quite that person anymore."

That statement. That was the entire reason Dean had avoided seeing her again. He knew her, sure. Deeply. In a way that not many people could know a person. From childhood. That was a special thing. But because he had known her then didn't mean she hadn't changed.

Didn't mean *he* hadn't changed either. His deepest fear was that he had changed in ways that Mel would no longer like, no longer care for.

Staying away, not lingering where the past had a hold of him seemed like the better idea. Missed out on so much time and so many memories never made. If only he'd put his pride aside and come back… Or never left.

Dean took a swig of the whiskey and then held the bottle out to Mel.

She shook her head. "Can't drink on the job."

"You're not getting out of here for another couple of hours. Live a little."

"I'm not some stupid kid who falls for peer pressure."

She'd had the first drink between the two of them. She and her girlfriends had made vodka sodas at a sleepover, and she insisted on making one for Dean a few days before he turned fifteen. Now she was the one on the straight and narrow and he was the bad influence. Oh, how the tables had turned.

"Don't drink much anymore?" he asked.

"Who has time?"

"Girls keep you busy, huh?"

She chuckled and leaned back on her elbows, stretching out along the sleeping bag. "That is an understatement."

Dean focused on the food, swirling his wooden spoon around, scraping up burned bits. "Almost ready."

He sensed her eyes on him and had to remind himself not to stare. He hadn't always felt this way for her. In fact, they had spent the majority of their childhoods irritated that so many people dared assume they were dating.

But then puberty hit, and he couldn't help but fall for her. From the moment it happened, he quietly nursed his crush, hoping it would go away, or that she'd feel the same.

It hadn't.

Even now, with her strewn across his sleeping bag, he was having thoughts he didn't want to be having. They were different than the thoughts of a teenager. More tender and nuanced.

But still. Thoughts he shouldn't be having.

"All done." Dean spooned a serving into his camp bowl and handed it to Mel. "You use the bowl. I'll eat out of the pan."

"Who is with your girls when you're working?"

She swallowed the bite in her mouth. "My mom."

"How is Jenny doing?"

"Still kicking."

"And your dad."

Mel sighed. "Still kicking, only softer."

"Ah. They do that, don't they?" Dean started pushing his food around the pan, trying to gain the courage to take a bite.

She looked at the bottle of whiskey. "Okay, I think I need a drink now."

"But you're on duty," he deadpanned.

Mel couldn't help laughing. "I need something to wash this dry chicken down."

Dean started to hand the bottle over and pulled it out of her reach before she could take it. A light tease. "My cooking isn't dry."

"Your cooking, no. The chicken that comes from a can?" Mel swiped the fifth from his hand easily. "Yes."

Dean watched her take a swig from the bottle. A dribble slid down her chin and made his stomach drop.

She handed him the bottle then wiped her chin with the back of her hand and looked into the bowl. "It's good, Dean. Really. Thank you."

He cleared his throat. "You're welcome."

"You're probably the best kind of trespasser I could have run into tonight."

"Really? Because I really thought you might shoot me."

Mel gave him a shit-eating grin. "I considered it. I'm pretty sure the department would have backed me up when I said it was justified." She pushed her spoon around the bowl. "It hurt me when you left the way you did."

A roll of thunder rattled the room, punctuating the pain she must have felt.

"I was feeling a little lost back then," he said. "I needed to figure some things out."

Her face hardened for a brief second before she laughed lightly. "Must be a male trait."

Dean looked away and gave up on eating at the way his stomach turned. Mark had abandoned her, too. "How about some music?"

"Sure."

He rifled through the bag once more, pulling out a portable radio. Like the good old days. He scanned for their favorite station.

"If you want alternative, you have to go to the classic rock station."

He raised an eyebrow. "Is that so?"

"We're getting old, Dean. Pearl Jam is classic now."

"Classic, huh? All right then."

Somehow that word felt apt to this moment to Dean. Hanging out in a forbidden place, the two of them, breaking the rules. This was classic Mel and Dean.

He'd hold onto that as long as he could.

Chapter Seven

The rain had started to ease as the evening wore on. According to dispatch, rescue still had their hands full but the chief had been in contact with a company who would be out to fix the road so Mel could leave soon.

"I can't believe you weren't going to at least stop by and say hi," she said as Dean fiddled with his camera.

"Would you have pulled a gun on me if I showed up at your house?" Dean asked.

Mel laughed and stretched her legs out on the sleeping bag. She'd made herself at home. "Perhaps."

He smiled and then asked a question that had been tugging at his thoughts. "Do you miss him?"

"No," she answered definitively.

"You can tell me the truth, Mel. You know you've always been able to tell me the truth."

"Telling someone the truth requires trust. You're telling me I should trust you now after ten years of no contact? You clearly don't know what it means to be betrayed."

"I didn't leave town to betray you."

"But it hurt."

"That doesn't mean it's a betrayal."

Mel laughed bitterly. "You missed out on ten years of my life—my children being born, the mill closing, and Mark leaving me. You think my best friend not being there or even dropping a note isn't a betrayal?"

Dean raised his brows. "Okay. Fair. If he came back—"

"He's not coming back."

"But if he did, would you try again?"

She shook her head. She'd played out that question in her mind before. And as each year passed, the betrayal of Mark's abandonment went deeper and deeper. "No. He doesn't deserve me."

Dean smiled and nodded. "Good for you."

She flushed, not willing to acknowledge how nice those words sounded coming out of his mouth. "What about you?"

"Hm?"

"Any love in your life?"

Mel had thought through this many times. In her head Dean had been hopping from town to town with girls in every city to call up should he need a good time. "I bet you left a trail of broken hearts behind you."

Dean crossed his arms over his chest and looked away. "You remember me in high school. I was a complete outcast. If you hadn't been around, I'd have been a complete loner."

"That's not true. There were plenty of times you ditched me to hang out with your guy friends."

He licked his lips. "Sure. I've had fun, but I never met anyone special. No one I'd want to settle down with. I've looked. I'm sure she's out there." He met her gaze and held it as some strange underlying current filled the room. "Somewhere."

When Dean had left, he'd been free to do as he pleased. Mel never had the chance. While she loved her kids, she couldn't help the bitterness that had started creeping in. Seeing him, with his obligation-free lifestyle, didn't help. Even before he left, he was always wandering around with his camera, trying to find the beauty in something, anything that would prove life was worth living.

She'd long ago shed the feeling that she was an outcast. Being a mom and a cop had grounded her. She could see in his eyes that he still felt lost. That made her sad for him. Dean would always hold a special place in her heart. Even if they didn't talk the rest of their lives.

Because of that bond, Mel's gut told her he wasn't saying everything. And she wanted to know that deeply secret little thought he was dancing around. "Are you actively looking for someone? Because if you found her, you'd probably have to stop living on the road."

He sighed. Instead of pressing for an answer, she let the silence do that for her.

"Okay. Fine." Dean sat up straighter and found her gaze. Hardened his jaw. "I've never found someone because no one has ever measured up to the way I feel about you."

Mel blinked and tilted her head, certain she'd misheard. "What?"

He looked away. "It's stupid."

His words sank in, but she couldn't make sense of them. "*What?*"

"Don't tell me you didn't know."

"No, I had no idea. You never told me. How could I—"

He cut her off with a soft laugh. "I was totally in love with you, Mel. I thought you felt the same until—"

Her heart was alternately swelling and breaking. The admission, so pure and strong, was giving her hope. And at the same time, she'd missed all the signs. Missed his love somehow, so caught up in her own dramas, and lost all this time.

"You were my best friend. And then you and Mark started dating and he was, you know, everything I wasn't. Richer. More popular. And then—"

"And then I got pregnant right before graduation."

Dean pursed his lips. "I'd deluded myself into thinking I was okay with that. But the closer the wedding came…" His shoulders collapsed. "You were so happy, and I knew there was never going to be a chance for me. So I left."

"You never told me how you felt."

He raked his hand over his short hair. "I know it was my fault, trust me."

Mel's eyes bubbled with tears. It was her fault, too. As she had fallen deeper in love with Mark, he hurt her more and more. He was never as good to her as she wanted him to be, as good as he acted in the beginning. And all the while, Dean had stuck by her side. Though she was in a relationship with Mark in name, she was in love with Dean. That was her secret, too. One she'd never told anyone. "I...loved you too."

"I know you did," he said, accepting it as a concession.

"No, Dean." Mel touched her chest. "I loved you like *that*. Like you're saying."

Dean furrowed his brow.

"I was in so deep with Mark and then—" She closed her eyes causing a tear to drip down her cheek. "My girls are my everything. I don't regret being with Mark."

"I know you don't."

She shrugged. "But I wanted you. By the time I got pregnant, I mean, I didn't think there was any way to...you deserved more than me."

Dean frowned. "That's ridiculous."

"I was having another guy's baby."

"And I was crazy with jealousy."

Mel felt like she was witnessing a tragedy unfold. Had she known that Dean felt the same, she would have taken the risk and told him how she felt. "I didn't want to ruin our friendship."

"I know. Me either."

"I didn't think you could ever feel the same."

"I know, Mel. I get it." Dean sat beside her on the sleeping bag. "I'm a coward."

"You're not."

"I am."

"Then I am, too."

He tentatively reached for her face and pushed her hair from her cheek. "Maybe we both are."

As he drew his hand back, she grabbed his wrist and pushed the palm of his hand to her cheek. She wanted all this time to count for something. She kissed his palm softly and then blinked away the sting of her tears.

He sighed happily. Then, he leaned in and pressed his lips to hers.

Mel had imagined Dean's kiss since she was in high school. She wasn't exactly sure when her feelings for him started to shift from friend to something more, but they had. And it'd thrown her for a loop. Sometimes she'd wondered if she should ask him to kiss her so she could get that first kiss out of the way.

She had never stopped wanting it.

Chapter Eight

Mel's kiss was better than Dean had ever dreamed or hoped. Her lips were soft and tender, her teeth teased his lower lip, and her tongue flicked into his mouth playfully. She rested her hands against his chest. His heart beat even harder at her touch.

He pulled away and lightly held her face in his hands. Her cheeks were blushed. So beautiful.

She let out a small moan. "Well, that was worth waiting for."

"I'm glad you think so." He twisted a lock of her damp hair. He wanted to make her moan like that again, wanted to hear all the sounds that came out of her when he made her feel good. If she would let him, he would do everything in his power to make her feel good.

He kissed her forehead softly and let his lips linger there. She smoothed her hands from his chest to his back, pulling herself closer to him. "Oh, Dean…"

"Mel..."

She sighed into his neck, sending a shiver down his spine.

"I hope you know I'm not letting you go tonight," he murmured. "Now that I have you, I can't."

"I wouldn't want it any other way."

He had forgotten how petite she was. Her feistiness always made her seem ten feet tall. Now, though, in his arms, she seemed so small. Needed to be protected. And he had always felt right for the job.

Even if it was only for one night, he was determined to be there for her.

She lifted her head and stroked his facial hair. His heart nearly burst through his chest at her gentle touch. Mel had been there from the beginning. The life they'd lived while younger had made him the man he had grown into. How could he not love her so completely and utterly? For all his life?

"I don't want to make you feel like you have to do anything," he whispered.

She grinned. "That's nice, but I never do what I don't want to."

He leaned into her and kissed her lips softly. "I want you, Mel."

He felt her breath hitch, which added fuel to his desire. Slowly, he ran his hands from her shoulders to her waist, over her hips, and around the fullness of her behind. "You're so beautiful."

"Dean..."

He grabbed her hips and held her as he nudged his erection against her. "I want to make love to you." He kissed her again. "Can I do that?"

Mel sighed before whispering. "I'm on duty."

He trailed kisses down her jaw to her neck.

"It'd be...so bad if anyone found out that not only was I hanging out with a trespasser..."

"Mm-hmm."

She pressed into him. "But that I was also fraternizing with him."

His lips moved to her collarbone. He slipped his fingers under the hem of the sweatshirt she was wearing.

"I could lose my job," she whispered but did nothing to stop him. In fact, she dug her fingers into his hair.

"Yeah, you could." He lightly teased her skin with his fingertips. "I should probably stop so you don't get into trouble."

She wrapped her hand around his chin. She pressed her nose and forehead to his. "If you stop now, I'll never speak to you again." She kissed him hungrily and pulled him on top of her.

Dean tugged the sweatshirt up, revealing her bare breasts. She grabbed his hands and pressed them to her, moaning as he kneaded her flesh. He found her mouth with his and pressed their lips together. She deepened the kiss and any hesitation he might have had faded.

For ten years, Dean had imagined this moment. He needed her. And he needed her now.

He pulled at the sweatpants he'd loaned her. "Take these off."

She did as he said and lifted her hips enough to remove the pants. As she removed her pants, he quickly undressed and then reached into his bag. He felt around until he found a condom, which he quickly tore open and put into place. Now naked, she gasped and grabbed the front of his shirt, pulling his lips back into hers. As their mouths dueled, Dean pressed his body into hers. Each movement of his hips elicited a moan from Mel.

She took hold of him and guided the head to her entrance. "Please?"

He pushed his hips forward and groaned as she dug her fingers into his back. Each pulse of their hips was accompanied by a wave of pleasure inside him that compounded upon itself. Eventually, he was unable to keep silent, grunting with every stroke.

Mel wrapped her legs around his hips, taking him deeper, hanging onto him as he worked himself inside of her.

Their moans tangled together with the static of the radio and the torrent of rain outside.

He gripped the sleeping bag on either side of her head. Her body began to shake and pulse, her hips moving without rhythm.

"Look at me," Dean grunted.

She opened her eyes as she held onto him tightly, digging her hands into his shoulders. She cried out as she stiffened beneath him. The aftershocks of her orgasm were accompanied by small pulses of her hips, making his body shudder. By the time he was done, there was absolutely nothing left in him.

He collapsed on top of her, breathless. "Holy shit."

She rubbed his back softly and kissed the crown of his head. "You all right?"

There weren't any words for how good Dean felt. Every nerve in his body was sparkling like water caught in the sunlight. He had forgotten how nice being close to a person like this felt.

And at the same time, he'd never so well and truly given himself over to someone like this.

"I'm sorry we..." Dean said through heaving breaths. "I would have liked to do this somewhere more proper."

Mel laughed. "I don't think there would have been anywhere more proper for us than here, Dean."

There was something true to that. They had never been conventional. Always running wild, always doing things askew.

Why wouldn't they have sex in the foreman's office of the abandoned mill? He traced the line of her jaw, pushing his thumb to her lip. In an instant, she was no longer a nearly thirty-year-old mother of two and an upstanding police officer, but the wild and carefree young woman he used to know. With her hopeful smile and bright eyes, he was transported in time.

His heart broke for all the time they had lost. But he also knew not everyone got a second chance like this.

Chapter Nine

Climbing out of the sleeping bag in the morning was painful. Not only was the morning tinged with after-rain cold, but Mel had also fallen in love with the feeling of being tangled in Dean's arms.

She had no idea when a rescue vehicle would be out to get her and had slept fitfully, wondering if at any moment another police cruiser would pull up.

On the other hand, Dean was a heavy sleeper. He didn't snore or toss and turn. He'd slept like a log.

Her clothes had mostly dried, though they looked warped and in need of a wash and press. In the foreman's bathroom, Mel tried to make herself look presentable. Surely, no one would suspect she'd had a night full of heartfelt admissions and sex.

She rearranged the chunks of her blonde hair and sighed. A shower. That's what she really needed when she got home. And a meal that hadn't come from a can.

When she emerged fully dressed and her holster in place, she wandered back over to the sleeping bag and jostled Dean awake. "Hey," she cooed, tenderly ran her fingers over his brown hair.

He blinked awake. "What time is it?"

"Early. You can keep sleeping, but I wanted to say goodbye first."

"What?" He pushed himself up onto his elbow.

The sleeping bag fell, revealing the top of his chest and the soft hair on it that she'd woven her fingers in. On his left pec, there was a tattoo Mel hadn't gotten a good look at the night before. He had many more tattoos than the single one he'd had when he left Cloverton. She'd been with him when he'd gotten it. He cried like a baby as the artist made a small fir tree on his ankle. She'd laughed while she held his hand.

Now, he had a sleeve of leaves and flowers that spread onto his chest. Must have taken years to complete. And it suited him and his love of nature.

"I'm going to head out front and wait for my ride."

"Right, but I..." He reached out and touched her arm. "When can I see you again?"

Her heart ached. It was nice that he wanted to see her again, but she knew the score, even if he wasn't ready to accept it. He was a loner and would be hitting the road soon. She was a mom to two kids who needed stability. There was no future in this. "Aren't you leaving soon?"

"I was planning on it but after last night, I'm not ready to be away from you again."

She couldn't argue with that. After their first round, they had spent a long time talking about his adventures before making love again, softer the second time.

They meshed together like interlocking puzzle pieces that had been searching for each other. Mel had never felt so in sync with someone, not even with her ex-husband.

However, she had no illusions about what the morning would bring. Dean, while potentially well-intentioned, had a life and a career to get back to. And so did she. She had her job, she had the girls, and she still had to figure out how to pay for their soccer camp.

She cupped his face in her hand. "You gotta get out of here, all right? I can't cover for you. It's not in my blood anymore."

Dean's frown dissipated, leaving his eyes sullen. "Yeah. Right."

"Part of the job."

"Of course. It was...fun," he said with a forced smile.

Mel nodded. "Yeah. It was." Though she knew better, she gave him a soft kiss, for old times' sake.

They were interrupted by the grating sound of the roll-top door. "Mel?"

She pulled away from Dean and looked toward the office door. "Shit," she whispered. "It's Chet."

"Chet?"

"My partner on the force. I have to go."

He was not acting as urgently as her, panning his gaze to the door and then back to her. "Yeah. You do."

Then, he yanked her into his arms once more, giving her a deep, passionate kiss. One she'd remember.

"I'll be back."

Mel patted his shoulder softly. "Sure you will."

"Mel!" Chet yelled.

She pushed herself up and rushed out of the office, not even giving him a parting look. "Hey!"

Chet looked up at her from the mill floor. "Jeez, you look terrible!"

"Huh, wonder why?" Mel shot back, descending the metal staircase.

He nodded toward the office. "Make yourself comfortable?"

She swallowed. *Don't look guilty. Sell it.* "Warmer up there than down here. More insulated. Fewer mice. Come on. I'm more than ready to get out of here."

As she walked with Chet out of the warehouse, Mel didn't dare look back. She didn't dare wonder what was going through Dean's mind or if he was watching her as she left.

She had spent the past ten years learning to live without him. A little hiccup like this didn't mean all that progress was lost. So what if it was ten more years? Twenty? She'd survive.

Outside, Chet's cruiser was parked on the side of the road. He'd been able to walk the causeway fine. As he explained that a road crew would be coming by in about an hour to patch up the bridge, Mel prayed Dean would be out of there by then.

When Mel arrived home, no one was happy to see her. Ellie was still angry about missing her playdate the night before, Hannah was working on a loose tooth that wasn't coming out, and Mel's mother, Carol, could tell something was up.

"You're too cheerful for having spent the night in the mill," Carol said, narrowing her eyes.

Mel wouldn't describe her mood as cheerful, but she certainly was more upbeat than she should have been given the circumstances. There was a spring in her step. She hadn't had sex in four years. Of course she felt good. "It was kind of like camping."

"You've never been camping," Carol said.

"Yeah, we've *never* been camping," Ellie said from her place in front of the television next to her sister where they were watching cartoons.

Carol lifted a brow with her usual accusatory stare. Mel had always felt like a slight disappointment to her mother. She wasn't the girly girl her mom wanted, and she got pregnant out of wedlock by a man her mother didn't like. It didn't matter that Mel had given her two beautiful grandchildren she adored and had made a life for herself. Carol always seemed to want a little bit more than Mel was able to give.

Consequently, Mel never wanted to ask for anything. Her mom and dad, while frugal people, would be willing to make up the difference for soccer camp. But Mel's obstinate pride got in the way of that.

"I should go shower," Mel said. "Thanks for taking care of the girls all night, Mom. Means a lot."

She saw her mother out the door and then went to the couch, leaning over behind the girls with a smile. "So what's the plan for today?"

"I dunno," Ellie said.

Hannah smiled at her mother. "Cartoons."

"I can see that. But we're not going to watch cartoons all day, are we?"

"Why not?" Ellie asked with a cool tone. "I'm stuck in this house so there's nothing better to do."

Mel opened her mouth to reply but was cut off by her cell phone ringing. She pulled it out of her pocket and recognized the number immediately. *Net Stars.* "You know our rules, Ellie. You shouldn't have even asked at the last minute."

Her logic was met with a dramatic sigh.

Nine years old and already giving attitude. Mel would have to figure out how to nip this in the bud. Maybe Chet had some advice. That would have to be saved for later though. Mel stepped into the kitchen and answered the phone in a low voice. "Hello?"

"Ms. Hart?"

"Yes, that's me."

"Oh, good! This is Georgia, from Net Stars. I'm so happy you picked up. I wanted to—"

"I know I'm behind on the payment," Mel said softly. "I promise I will have it ready to go by the end of the week. Please don't give up their spots."

"Actually, I was calling to confirm we received the rest of your balance and verify the email where I should send a materials list so that Ellie and Hannah are prepared for their first day of camp."

Mel frowned. "Sorry, the balance has been paid?"

"Yes. All taken care of."

Mel didn't understand. Had Chet gone behind her back and paid off the balance? Had the girls said something to her mother? None of this made sense. "Who gave you the outstanding balance?"

The woman laughed awkwardly. "Um. I'm not sure. I didn't take the payment. That happens through our accounting department. I just do outreach on the kids attending."

"Okay. Well. Good."

"We're excited to have Ellie and Hannah in the program."

"Yes, they are excited too. Thank you." She confirmed her email, though she was still trying to work out who would have made the payment.

Mel hung up and immediately called Chet, peeking into the living room to make sure the girls were still occupied.

"Mel, what's up?"

"Did you pay off my balance to Net Stars?"

"What?"

"Did you pay for the girls' soccer camp?"

"Thought about it, but no. I know you can handle it."

She looked around the kitchen but wasn't seeing her surroundings. "Well, apparently someone paid it for me. And I don't know who it could have been."

Mel froze. *No. It couldn't be.*

"Well, I promise it wasn't me. Maybe your mom and dad."

"Maybe." Mel knew in her gut who it was. She didn't know how he figured out that she needed help, but apparently he had. Dean. That was the only person who made sense.

Mel didn't remember mentioning Net Stars or anything like that, but maybe she did. Lots of things slipped out while they were talking that she probably didn't remember. They were overshadowed by the bigger admission of the evening. "Anyway. Sorry. Thought I'd ask."

"No problem. Glad to hear it's all worked out though."

At the end of the day, that was the most important thing. "Yeah. Me, too." The girls would get to go to their soccer camp, and Mel wouldn't have to worry about fronting the money.

Someone had already taken care of it.

After hanging up with Chet, Mel pulled up her email. Sure enough, a materials list had been sent to her. Shin guards, mouth guards, cleats... The girls had everything on the list. Thank goodness, but they would need to double-check the condition, sizes, and—more importantly—make sure they could even find what they already had.

"Girls," Mel called out as she came back into the living room, "get your soccer stuff together while I take a shower. We need to see what to buy before camp starts."

Ellie and Hannah finally pulled their attention away from their TV. Both wore big grins.

"And then we can go play some soccer in the park. How's that sound?"

The girls cheered in response and cuddled into Mel. Being a single mom was hard most of the time, but this made it all worth it.

Twenty-four hours ago, Mel had no idea that Dean Gorman was going to walk back into her life. Now, she couldn't imagine what would have happened if he hadn't.

Her only regret was she had no way to thank him. No phone number, no address.

So, she thought long and hard, hoping against every hope that somehow, he'd feel what she was thinking.

Thanks, Dean. I owe you one.

Chapter Ten

Dean had gone ten years without Mel. Ten years without her resounding laugh and attitude. Ten years without Cloverton. Sure, he had thought about her all the time, checked in on her life, and wondered what would have happened if he hadn't run away. But life went on. He'd developed his photography career, traveled the world, and took the time he needed to find himself. At least as much as he could without the woman he'd always loved by his side.

Ten years.

All it took was one night with Mel to bring it all back.

Leaving her and Cloverton again proved harder than he'd anticipated. In the week since he'd climbed on his bike and driven out of town, he couldn't stop wishing he'd never left.

It didn't make sense.

Before, he hadn't known that the feeling of love and affection was mutual. He couldn't wrap his mind around how Mel could walk away from what they'd discovered, what they'd shared without even trying to give it more of a shot.

In the time since he'd left, he edited the photos and did a small write-up on each one so his assistant could get the photos organized and help him select which ones to use for his project. He'd managed to work with his agent to sell some older photos and had started narrowing down the options for his next project.

What he hadn't managed to do was get Mel off his mind. He replayed the events of that night over and over. And the morning when she hurried out after a rushed goodbye.

More importantly, without giving him a chance to give her his phone number. Without the chance of getting hers.

Which was why Dean decided he had to go back to Cloverton.

And this time, he wouldn't avoid the town or the people in it. He'd face his past dead on. It wasn't going to be pretty, but it was going to be...worth it.

He parked his motorcycle in front of The Treasure Chest, a women's boutique that was a new addition to the Main Street storefronts. Other than that, and a few empty windows, it was mostly the same.

He had expected Main Street to be rundown and dilapidated, like the mill. Instead, against all odds, it was thriving.

But the people seemed different.

Except that they were as nosy as ever though. He could feel eyes on him from every direction and could almost hear the whispers. But he got it. He had left abruptly. Of course, there would be chatter at his unannounced return.

Keep calm. Just get a coffee and head out.

Dean crossed to The Coffee Nut. He lamented that he didn't know Mel's coffee order but thought he might be able to guess. She always liked sweet things. Maybe a fancy, overdressed iced mocha would do the trick.

As soon as he walked into the coffee shop, he was greeted with the smiling face of Ryan Carter.

"Well, well, well. Look what the cat dragged in."

Dean grinned. "How's it going, Carter?"

The two had played on the basketball team together for one season after Dean's father forced him to join to try to make more friends. It hadn't worked. "I feel as if I've seen a ghost."

"You wouldn't be the first to say so."

Ryan leaned on the counter. "What are you doing back in town?"

Dean breathed a sigh of relief knowing that Mel hadn't run around telling everyone about his adventures. That was the last thing he needed. On top of already being the prodigal son. "Just visiting."

"It's about time. We've missed you around here."

"Well," Dean said with a shrug, "my parents retired to Arizona, so not much reason to return."

Ryan nodded. "What can I get you?"

"A black coffee and a—"

"Let me guess. Iced peppermint latte. Maybe an extra shot since it's the afternoon slump."

Confusion clouded his mind. "Huh?"

"That's Mel's order. You're here to see her, right?"

Dean's heart tightened. "Yeah. How'd you know?"

"Gee, I don't know, Gorman. You haven't been back to town in a decade, and you don't have any family left. The only thing that makes sense is you're here to visit Mel."

"Guess I'm predictable." Dean ran his hand over his freshly trimmed beard. He wanted to look clean. Put together. So he'd taken his time at the motel to shower and shave.

Ryan set to work on making the coffee. "Fair warning, though. She'll probably bite your head off. She was pretty pissed when you left before her wedding."

She already has. "Sounds like Mel."

But he was there to make amends. And hopefully, start anew.

Thanks to the one conversation Dean had overheard between Chet and Mel, he knew exactly where Mel would be today. Luckily the field was within walking distance of the coffee shop. Riding a motorcycle while holding two coffees wasn't a magic trick he had learned yet.

The Net Stars website had been bookmarked on his phone from the moment Mel abandoned him at the mill. He saw the price tag and realized why it had stressed Mel out. It was a lot for two kids, but if their dad wasn't such a deadbeat, it shouldn't have been a problem. Dean pulled out a card and made the payment. Mel deserved a break and if this was the only way he could give her one, he'd take it.

The girls had a game and, if he was correct, Mel would certainly have moved hell and high water to be there to support them.

At the Cloverton Elementary field, there were two scrimmages going on with parents lined up on either side. Some were standing, getting way too involved with the game for their own good, others had come prepared for a long day with their collapsible chairs.

Though Mel wasn't the tallest of the bunch, he could spot her anywhere.

Although it helped that she was standing next to her partner. Chet was cheering along with the other parents making Dean think he had a kid on the field, too.

Dean tightened his grip on the coffee and tried to take measured steps toward the field. Consequently, he moved like an unsure kid trying to jump into a round of double Dutch.

He stopped briefly to watch the ongoing games. The older kids on one half, the tikes on the other. Though he'd only seen Mel's daughters in pictures, it was obvious which ones they were. Towheaded and scrappy on the field with the younger one being a little too rambunctious.

"Defense, Hannah!" Mel yelled through cupped hands.

Chet laughed and patted her on the back.

Deep breath. Get in there.

Dean made his way over to Mel, ignoring any sidelong glances from parents who recognized him.

Chet saw him first, eyebrows raised and jutting his chin toward him in an intimidating greeting. "Hey, man."

Mel turned with a smile on her face. That smile immediately fell upon seeing Dean. "Hey."

"Hi. Good to…" Dean gave her an awkward one-armed hug, clocking how stiff Mel was in his embrace. "Good to see you." He held up the drinks. "Brought you coffee."

Mel opened her mouth to say something, but nothing came out. Probably resisting the urge to demand to know what the hell he was thinking showing up unannounced.

"Carter told me your order." Dean handed it to her.

"Thanks," Mel said, but didn't make a move to sip the drink.

He suddenly regretted his plan. She wasn't acting cold toward him, but she was acting strange. Clearly, she was surprised by his unexpected presence, but he couldn't be sure she wasn't offended.

"Dean, this is Chet. My partner at the station."

Dean and Chet exchanged a nod. "Nice to meet you," Dean said, hoping Chet didn't remember him from his misspent youth.

"Hey."

The silence that followed made Dean almost certain there was more going on here besides partners.

"Chet's son plays with Ellie, my eldest." Mel gestured toward the field of older kids.

"Oh, that's nice."

The parents erupted in cheers from all sides. Dean took his attention back to the field of younger kids.

"Pinnies win!" someone shouted.

Dean immediately spotted Mel's youngest barreling toward her with wide open arms. Her big smile revealed several missing teeth.

"Well, how about that?" Mel handed her coffee to Chet, and then wrapped her daughter into a humongous hug and lifted her up like she weighed nothing. "Good job, baby!"

"Did you see how I ran back and forth so many times?" the little girl asked.

"I did! I could barely keep up. You were like a ping pong ball."

The girl threw her head back with laughter.

Dean felt edged in sadness. He'd only heard Mel talk about her kids and seen pictures here and there. Seeing his childhood best friend *being* a mother was a strange reality. He'd always known Mel would make a good mom from how she took care of him so many times back in the day. But the fact she could put on a big smile and celebrate her child despite everything she'd been through made her a rockstar in his eyes.

"Mommy..."

"What is it?"

The girl eyed Dean skeptically, lips twisting to the side, and then pressed her mouth against Mel's ear. Mel glanced at Dean and took a deep breath. "Hannah, this is my friend Dean."

"Hi, Hannah," he said with a tentative smile. He hadn't spent a lot of time with children. His only goal was to never make them cry by being too big and scary.

"Dean and Mommy went to school together for a long time. We were friends."

Best friends.

"Like me and Gemma."

"Like you and Gemma, yeah," Mel said. "Can you say hi?"

"Hi," Hannah said, clinging to Mel.

Mel hitched her daughter up higher on her hip. "Well, we should go watch your sister finish up her game." Her blue eyes notched into Dean's with precision. "Good to see you."

No, no, no. Dean had not come all the way out here for nothing. He'd picked an inappropriate time to show up. He understood that now. But no way in hell was he letting Mel walk away from him. Not again. "Wait, before you go, I'm in town for a few days. We should get dinner. Tonight."

His words came out like vomit, but he needed to get the point across given how fast Mel was ready to step away.

"I don't think so, Dean, I have the girls and—"

"Why don't they come over for dinner with us? Playdate with Erik. They've been begging for one," Chet said with a cheerful grin.

Mel glared at him over her shoulder. "That's nice, Chet, but—"

"Playdate! Playdate!" Hannah started to chant. "Playd—"

"Shh. Hannah, you are yelling right in my ear," Mel admonished. Her jaw hardened.

Damn it, he'd stressed her out.

"One dinner couldn't hurt," Dean said, though his confidence was fading.

"Yeah, Mommy! One dinner couldn't hurt," Hannah repeated.

Dean pointed at her playfully. "I like her."

"I like you, too." She laughed in response.

"Fine. Okay," Mel gave in. "*Early* dinner. I want to be home by eight."

"Can do," Dean said with a smile.

Chet tapped Mel on the shoulder. "Thirty seconds, Mel!"

"Oh no! We'll miss it!" Hannah cried out, wriggling out of Mel's arms.

"You two go ahead," Mel said, waving them toward the other field. "I'll be right there."

Chet and Hannah rushed over to watch the last seconds of Ellie's game. Finally, what Dean had wanted. A moment alone with Mel.

"It's not the best idea to show up unannounced when I'm with my kids, Dean."

Dean laughed limply. "Well, I didn't have your number, don't know where you're living, so... I guess I didn't have much of a choice."

"You had a choice," Mel said coldly. "You could have stayed away."

He felt as though he'd been turned to stone by her words.

She pursed her lips. "Family Time Café at five o'clock. It's where Buck's used to be."

Buck's was the old diner. He'd driven past Family Time Café on the way in. He missed the big road sign with the antlers sticking out of it but was glad to see the building still standing. "Got it."

She nodded before walking off to join Chet and Hannah without a word. It might not have been a happy reunion like he'd hoped, but he still had a chance. A chance to prove to Mel that he was back. For good, if she'd have him.

Chapter Eleven

Timing had never been Mel's strong suit, and tonight was no different. She was late as usual. But she had a really good excuse—she didn't want to be here. She didn't want to have this conversation. Being a cop didn't mean she enjoyed confrontation. She dreaded it, especially with Dean.

He already had a table when she arrived. He started to get up to greet her, but Mel hustled herself into the chair across from him.

"I tried to get the one in the corner, but I figured we had grown out of sitting by the bathroom," Dean chuckled.

Mel glanced over at the corner table where a couple of high school-aged kids were loitering. That used to be their table. People would come and go through the afternoon while Mel and Dean held court with their milkshakes and potato skins.

"What's good here?" Dean asked, reaching for his menu.

The food was better now, but nothing could live up to the atmosphere of Buck's. Sure the old diner had always been dirty and grimy, but it was charming. Since Family Time Café opened, Mel had found it sterile and trendy in a social media way.

"Everything," Mel said softly, opening her menu.

Dean looked down at the options and chewed on his lip. For such a big man, he sure knew how to look unsure of himself. The thought sent a wave of emotion through Mel. She didn't want to hurt Dean, but she had boundaries that needed to be enforced.

"Thanks for meeting me," he said without looking up.

"I kind of didn't have a choice."

His gray eyes focused on hers. "Would you have come if Chet hadn't been there to offer to take the girls?"

"No."

He gave her a half-grin that caused her entire body to warm. "Liar."

Not the butterflies in her stomach. Not this flirtation. She couldn't handle this right now. Her plate was full and she didn't need anything else added to it. "What are you doing back, Dean?"

"I wanted to see you."

"Why?"

Hurt filled his eyes. "Why is that hard to believe?"

"Uh, I don't know, ten years of nothing?"

He dropped the menu on the table. "I've apologized for that. I even explained why I left. I thought we were moving on."

A waitress blew by with a huge tray of dishes, calling over her shoulder to them, "I'll be with you in a second."

Mel couldn't muster a reply. Her heart was doing a crazy dance in her chest that was causing her brain to short-circuit. Thoughts wouldn't seem to form. Dean started talking to her again, but she couldn't hear him over her brain replaying the night they'd made love. And the heartbreak she'd felt when he left town once again.

Not that she hadn't been anticipating it. She'd even told him to go. But part of her had wanted him to stay. A big part. But he hadn't. He'd disappeared. Again. Like every man she'd ever cared about.

"You all right, Mel? Did you hear anything I said?"

"I'm sorry, I'm a bit distracted."

Dean raised an eyebrow but nodded. "Okay. Maybe we should wait to order food before we talk."

"Tell me why you're here," Mel said, gesturing for him to be quick about it. The faster he came out with it, the faster she could get out of there. And go home to her kids where she belonged.

"I'm here for you. Because I miss you. Because I want us to try to... I want us to give this thing between us a try."

Mel shook her head. "That's insane."

"Why?"

"Because I'm not something to visit every now and then when you have a couple of days off and want to get laid."

His eyes widened and lifted his hands as if surrendering. "Woah, that's not what I'm trying to say. Not at all."

"Then explain."

"I'm trying to tell you I'm here to—"

"Hey, you two," the waitress said with a bright smile and tilt of her head. "Thanks for being patient. Can I get you started with a few drinks?"

Dean hesitated before answering. "I'll have the club sandwich and an iced tea. What do you want, Mel?"

She shook her head. "I'm not staying long enough to eat."

After a moment of staring her down, he smiled at the waitress. "I guess I'll get that to go."

"Sure thing," she said as if she finally picked up on the stress at the table. She gathered their menus and promised his meal would be out quickly. As soon as she was gone, Mel clutched her hands in her lap.

"I don't want fake promises and bullshit excuses, Dean. I don't need them."

"I'm not here to—"

"I have kids and bills and responsibilities. I'm a grown-up now."

He scoffed. "So am I, actually."

"Really? Galivanting around the country, sleeping in abandoned buildings, living on canned goods and a portable camp stove? None of those things make you grown."

"I've built a pretty good career doing those things."

"Good for you. But I have a family and you have no idea what it takes to provide for them."

He turned away, looking out the window. "Where is all this hostility coming from?"

"You disappear for a decade and after one night together, you think you have the right to drop in at my kids' soccer games. You don't have that right. You don't get to meet my kids and disrupt their lives. We had one night, and it was nice, but that doesn't give you the right to come and go as you please."

The hurt in his eyes returned and his shoulders sagged. "I'm sorry. I didn't mean to overstep. I'll be more aware in the future."

"There is no future, Dean," she said softly. "I'm not going down this road."

"What road?"

"The one where I watch you drive away without me. Without *us*. Because I'm an us now. And my kids have lost enough thanks to some man walking out on them. I won't put them through that again."

"I'm not like him."

"I think you are. I think you're exactly like him. Settling down, having a family, and raising kids sounds great in theory. But it's work. It's hard work. Every single day. It's exhausting and, to be frank, sometimes it's debilitating. Financially, emotionally, and mentally. Mark couldn't handle it. I don't think you can, either. I think you'll wake up one day and realize you are in over your head. And then you'll climb on your bike and ride off, leaving me and my girls brokenhearted."

"So I don't even get a chance? Because you think I can't handle it."

"I know you can't."

"I was young when I left last time."

Mel glanced around as she drew a deep breath. "Did you pay for their soccer camp?"

Dean didn't respond, but his silence told her what she needed to know. Taking an envelope from her purse, she pushed it to him. She'd scraped together every dollar she could find to pay him back.

"I don't want your charity," she stated sliding it closer to him.

Dean shook his head, refusing to take her money.

She simply left the envelope sitting there. "I know it might not feel like it, but this is what is best for everyone."

"Melanie," he stated firmly when she stood and started for the door.

She ignored him. If she didn't, he'd break through the paper-thin wall she was putting between them.

Dean slid from the booth and blocked her way. "Mel, I came here because I want to be with you. I haven't stopped thinking about you since I left town. I've been running from this place for so long, and I don't want to do that anymore." Tears rushed into his eyes. "I want to come home. I want to be with you."

She stared at him for a long moment before shaking her head. "It isn't only about me."

He hesitated before taking her hand. "I know. And I know it's sudden—"

"I don't do sudden anymore, Dean." Mel snatched her hand away from him. "I don't rush into things. And I don't take chances that could hurt my kids." She stepped around him and went out the door.

"Here's your order," the waitress said, almost in a whisper.

Dean dug in his pocket and pulled out a twenty. As he handed it to her, he recalled the envelope on the table. He snatched that and then accepted the food from the woman. "Have a good night," he muttered.

"You, too," she said in a singsong voice before walking away.

Dean rushed out of the diner, following Mel toward her old SUV. He caught the door before she slammed it shut. "Listen—"

"Damn it, Dean," she cursed, still trying to pull the door shut.

"We can take things slow. We can date. We don't have to rush."

She dropped her head back onto the seat and groaned. "Are you kidding me?"

"I know you're scared."

"Don't do this," she said looking at him.

"But I'm not Mark."

Mel scoffed, "Oh, please."

"I'm not."

"You were the *original* Mark."

Dean dropped his hand from the open door.

"You left first," she stated firmly, though her eyes were starting to well over. "You're the blueprint, not him."

The pain of a thousand daggers hit his heart. "I didn't... I didn't leave *you*." His voice creaked out of him. Broken.

"You did."

"I didn't."

"*You did*," she snapped. "The last time I saw you, I told you I was pregnant, and that Mark thought we should go to the courthouse and get married. I told you I didn't know if that's what I wanted. You told me he'd be a good husband. And then you walked away. You left for ten years." She stabbed her finger into his chest. "*You. Left. First.*"

Dean remembered that conversation vividly. He hadn't realized she was presenting him with the opportunity to step up for her. He would have. Or at least he'd have tried. "I'm sorry. I didn't mean to let you down. Let me prove myself to you now."

"No."

"Mel—"

"*No*. Men think they get to move on without any repercussions. You all think you get second chances. Where is *my* second chance?"

Dean wanted to shout that he was standing right in front of her. He'd be that for her. But he feared that would fall on deaf ears. Instead, he looked at her. Took her in. Every beautiful inch. His best friend since grade school. The only woman he'd ever loved.

"You don't want me," she said quietly. "You want the Mel you used to know. And, I'm so sorry, Dean, but I'm not..." Mel trailed off as tears slid down her face. "I'm not her anymore."

He desperately wanted to refute her, but she was right. She wasn't the same girl anymore. And he wasn't the same boy. They'd both grown up. He was foolish to think he could come back to Cloverton and everything would be as it had been ten years ago.

"I came here for you, Mel."

She shook her head slowly and tears reflected in her eyes. "Then leave for me, too."

Dean didn't have it in him to push any harder. He backed away from the car and watched the blue SUV reverse out of the parking spot and speed out of the lot.

After wondering *what if* for what seemed a lifetime, Dean had an answer. *What if* wasn't a question to be asked.

No longer *what if*, but *what could*.

What could happen now that things have been broken? What could grow if they both acknowledged the hurt and pain? What could they build together?

Dean had to stop going back in time.

He would be in the here and now. And he would take one last shot.

Chapter Twelve

"Looks like you've got a secret admirer," Chief Wilkes said when Mel walked into the station the next day.

Mel bristled. "What do you mean?"

Wilkes pointed with one of her carefully manicured fingers. "Roses."

Mel's eyes grew wide at the sight of the bouquet sitting on her desk. Beautiful, creamy pink roses. A dozen of them arranged perfectly. She didn't doubt this was the handy work of Jasmine Law, the florist at Dewy's Grocery Store. She'd always admired the flowers but could never justify such a frivolity when there were bills to be paid and mouths to feed.

Mel fished a small white envelope out of the center of the flowers, unsure if she wanted to open it.

"Hart's got a boyfriend," one of the young rookies said as he passed her desk.

"Shut it, Stevens," she shot back.

No boyfriend. Only a friend. She had pushed Dean squarely into that corner from the moment she drove out of the parking lot, refusing to give his promises and declarations one second of attention.

However, it was impossible to ignore them entirely. The idea that, after all this time, he was willing to give himself to her so fully was shocking. She'd be lying to herself if she said she wasn't at least toying with the idea in her imagination.

Read the damn thing, Mel. She ripped the envelope open with her thumb. A small note was scribbled on the gold-rimmed white card inside.

Let's take a drive like old times.

XO,

Dean

The *x* and the *o* were just two letters, but together their angles and curves hypnotized Mel. Her mind went back to the kisses and embraces she'd shared with Dean in the abandoned mill. A place so desolate burst with passion and life. Sometimes, on nights she could not sleep, she imagined their tangle and played it over and over in her head.

She'd love to do that again.

"Coffee?"

She looked up from the note to find Chet standing in front of her desk with her usual iced peppermint latte in his hand. "Oh, thanks," she said, taking it tentatively. "Always need coffee," she added taking a sip.

"Nice flowers."

She tossed the note down and gestured as if she was unfazed. "Yeah, they're pretty."

"They're from Dean, right?"

"Yeah. He's... He wants a chance with me but...I don't know. It's not worth talking about." Mel sat down at her desk and slid the bouquet to the right of her computer and then back again, trying to figure out where to put it so it was out of the way.

Chet leaned on the top of her cubicle, looking around to make sure he could speak candidly without Wilkes listening in on them. "Are you trying to run him off?"

Mel's attention snapped to her partner. "What?"

He eyed her. "He seems like a nice guy, but you seem determined to keep him away."

"I..." *No.* The answer was a firm no. If Dean left, then that meant the connection they had was truly severed. Maybe for good. All those desperate feelings of love and affection, the years of growing their love from friends to lovers to who knows what would have been all for nothing. Mel swallowed. "I don't know, Chet, it's not that simple."

"'Of course it isn't. But that's what relationships are like, aren't they? They're messy and complicated and take work." Chet paused. "But being complicated doesn't mean they can't feel easy."

Easy. What a perfect way to describe how it felt to be around Dean. Perhaps it had to do with their roots being intertwined from such a young age. Perhaps they were kindred spirits. Whatever it was, it worked.

After she had bristled against him in the mill, she gave in to him. And had the easiest, loveliest night of her life. Being with Dean could be easy.

"Why are you so against giving him a chance?" Chet asked.

"You're the one who is always trying to tell me not to accept shit from guys, aren't you?"

"Giving someone a chance doesn't mean taking their shit."

Mel chuckled. "Yeah, right."

"Look," Chet said growing serious, "I don't know all the details about what's happened between you two in the past. I only know bits and pieces and obviously...I'm *your* friend. I want you to be happy." He looked her in the eye. "And that means making sure you go for happiness when I see you're standing in your own way."

He had a point. She was the one standing in her own way when it came to Dean. She had become a pro at protecting herself in the wake of her ex's abandonment. So much so that it was hard to ever justify letting the wall down.

Hell, Mel wasn't sure if she'd *ever* let her walls down.

He put his hands up in surrender. "Anyway. What do I know?"

"Nothing, Hudson," she said with a crack of a smile.

"Actually, I do know one thing," he replied and pulled out a scrap of paper from his pocket.

Mel took it from him. A phone number.

"I know how to use our system to find phone numbers. This is his. Call him, Mel. At least give the guy a chance."

She wrapped her fingers around the paper. She already knew her answer. "You're a pain in the ass, Chet."

He gave her a wink. "I know."

Later that evening, Mel smiled when she caught Hannah looking at her with a wide grin. "What's up, buttercup?"

"You look pretty."

Mel smiled and thanked her daughter before checking her reflection in the mirror by the door where she was primping her hair. They had a second chance tonight. A chance for both of them to make things right.

She'd called Dean almost immediately after receiving his phone number from Chet. The relief in his voice was apparent, which echoed the relief she'd felt in her chest.

This was the right choice. She might not know where it would lead, but it was right for now.

"Mom, there's a motorcycle out front," Ellie called from the other room.

"Oh! That's him!" Mel rushed into the other room and grabbed her purse.

"You're not riding on that thing, are you?" Chet asked from his place in front of the television where he and Ellie had been playing a video game.

Mel grinned. "Yes, I am, *Dad*."

Chet shook his head. "Girls, don't take after your mother."

"I want to ride on a motorcycle," Hannah stated.

Mel laughed and kissed her daughter's head. "Maybe someday." Then, she opened the door.

Dean was already coming up the front walk. He stopped short upon seeing Mel.

The two of them looked at each other for a long moment.

"Hey."

"Hey."

"My mom's name is Melanie," Hannah informed him, peeking out from behind Mel.

Dean chuckled. "You're right. Hello, Melanie."

Ellie appeared at Mel's other side, nearly reaching up to her shoulder. "Mom, is that him?"

Mel had always been honest with her girls. They knew their dad had left and knew that they shouldn't expect him to come back. They knew where babies came from because God forbid, they make the mistakes Mel did, even if Ellie was more of a blessing than anything. And they knew she was going on a date with Dean.

Though they'd never met him, they had heard stories about all the wild antics their mom would get up to with her best friend when she was younger. "When I was your age..." the stories would start.

"Yes," Mel answered. "Can you say hi?"

Ellie smiled shyly. "Hi."

"You must be Ellie," Dean said, making his way up the steps of the house to the front door.

"Holy shit, you're tall!" Hannah squeaked.

"Hannah!" Mel scolded with an embarrassed glance toward Dean.

"Sorry! Holy *cow*!"

"I see you get your mouth from your mother," Dean said with a grin.

Mel felt her cheeks warm with a blush. "I try my best not to cuss in front of my kids."

"She's not good at holding her tongue," Ellie explained.

"Trust me, I know," Dean replied. "Maybe you can tell me a few other things about your mom? We can compare notes."

The most important thing in any man Mel dated would be his compassion toward the girls. She had a feeling Dean would be capable of that, but she would have to make sure he was okay with them always coming first. Tonight was his test. So she might as well treat it like one. "Do you want to come in and talk for a little bit before we go out?" Mel asked.

Dean's lifted his eyebrows in surprise, but he nodded. "I'd like that."

"Let's all go sit in the living room and get to know each other," Mel said with a hopeful smile. "Maybe you can give Dean a tour of the house, huh?"

"You can see our bedroom," Hannah said, grabbing Dean's hand. "We have bunk beds."

Ellie grunted. "Don't remind me."

"Oh, I'd love to see that," Dean said, following Hannah inside. He tossed a smile over his shoulder for Mel. Just for her.

This might be good, Mel thought to herself. *Correction: this* will *be good.*

Chapter Thirteen

By the time Dean and Mel left for their Cloverton adventure, Ellie and Hannah both had nicknames. Smirk and Blur, respectively.

Ellie was Smirk for her sassiness while Hannah was Blur since she never seemed to stop moving.

"All right, are you going to have a slumber party with the kids, or are you two going to get on your way?" Chet asked after an hour of Dean getting to know the girls.

Mel sheepishly apologized. "I owe you, Hudson."

"Naw, you don't. He does."

Dean gave a curt nod as they said goodbye to the girls and Chet.

"Been years since I've ridden this thing," Mel remarked as they neared his motorcycle.

Dean held out his helmet. "I remember the first ride I took you on."

"You didn't have your license yet," she grinned.

"Nope. Still don't."

He straddled the motorcycle and patted the cushion for Mel to get on. She stared him down.

"Oh, come on, that was a joke."

She cocked one brow at him. "Show me."

He pulled out his wallet and showed her the Class M stamp on his license. "What are you—a cop?"

Mel laughed and got onto the bike behind him. "Who would have thought after all the terror we caused, huh?"

"You gotta remember your roots," Dean said over his shoulder. "Hold on."

She wrapped her arms around his waist, relishing the closeness of his body again. In the pit of her stomach, all her nerves lit up. Partly from arousal, the other from their closeness.

"You ready?" Dean asked in a soft drawl.

"Let's ride."

Dean had an entire night planned out, starting with a redo of Family Time Café. This time, they sat in their old favorite booth, not minding how close they were to the bathroom.

Then a walk down Main Street. Dean was sad about how much it had changed, but Mel eased him into the strangeness with her bright laugh and occasional touch to his back. Being back felt better with Mel at his side. Instead of stares and whispers about a stranger in town, there were smiles and greetings. When they were teens, they rushed through town without a care in the world, not worrying if they got in the way or who they might offend.

Now, they were older and carried themselves differently.

Dean never realized how much he wanted this. To be in his hometown and feel different. And yet exactly the same.

With Mel at his side, these complicated feelings felt easy. Eventually, he had the courage to reach out and grab her hand. There was still so much to talk about and untangle, but he wanted her to know that he'd always loved her. To feel him.

She accepted his hand and held it as they walked the length of town, all the way to Centennial Park. In the twilight days of summer, the park was busy from sunup to sundown and today was no different. The sky was blusteringly orange and pink as the sun began setting.

"Can we talk about us?" Dean asked softly.

"Not here," Mel replied. "Somewhere else. Someplace with fewer prying eyes."

That place Mel had in mind was the quiet football field of Cloverton High. Not under the bleachers as they would have back in the day. Now they sat in the sun. Too old to hide.

"They replaced the goalposts, huh?"

"Naw, they slathered yet another coat of paint on them," Mel said as they sat in the middle of the bleachers.

Dean looked around the bare bleachers, imagining them being filled with people they went to school with. "I don't think I ever went to a game."

"That's not true. You just don't remember it."

"Oh right. That was the first time I got drunk."

"You nearly streaked. I had to tackle you."

"My dad was pissed when I got home."

"He wasn't pissed."

Dean snorted. "You knew my dad. He was always pissed."

Mel conceded with a sigh. "Well, it's not because he was actually angry. He was worried." She paused, leaning back on the bleacher and looking up at the sky. "Being a parent is hard. We all worry in different ways." She grew quiet for a few moments before looking at him. "What do you think would have happened if we'd figured this out sooner?"

Dean hummed thoughtfully. "I don't know. I probably never would have left Cloverton."

"Yeah."

"And you never would have married Mark."

Mel nodded.

"But then I wouldn't have traveled, and you wouldn't have—"

"The girls."

"Right."

She picked at her nails. "Sometimes I wish things had worked out differently, but then I remember everything and..."

"We can't regret it because of hindsight."

"I guess nothing is promised. Maybe we never would have known at all."

"Maybe."

"If I hadn't walked into the mill and found you there and there hadn't been a storm and—" Mel shook her head in disbelief. "So many things had to align to get us here."

Dean silently thanked the universe. So many things worked to get them here. He was going to make it count. "Everything I said yesterday stands. I want to give us a shot."

She gave him a sidelong glance. "What about your work?"

"I'll work less. I've made a lot of good money. I have savings to fall back on until I work it out."

"You'd have to travel."

"Well, yes, sometimes."

"I'd be left here. Alone again."

"But you wouldn't be alone, Mel," Dean replied in a tender voice. "Travelling occasionally doesn't mean I'd be abandoning you. It means, you'd get a break from me now and then," he said with a sweet smile.

She laughed lightly. "God knows I'll need that."

He brushed her hair back. "I would be here for you. And the girls. You wouldn't have to work so hard. You wouldn't have to worry so much."

She nodded slowly. "What happens if you change your mind?"

"I won't."

"Don't say that. You don't know that."

"What happens if *you* change *your* mind?" Dean retorted.

Mel shook her head. "I know I'm not the only one who could get hurt here, Dean, but you have to recognize that this isn't simply about you and me. I have kids to consider."

Dean's mouth dried out. "Okay, answer me one question. And that's going to be all I need to hear." He gulped. "Do you want to have a future with me?"

Mel was silent. Her face grew tight. He couldn't tell if that was a good or bad sign. Or somewhere in the middle.

"Of course, I do," she said softly.

His heart leaped into his mouth.

"But it's not that simple."

"No, it's not, but let's start there." He reached out and touched her hand, heartened when she didn't pull away. "I'm not gonna say I should marry you or anything—"

Mel laughed wryly.

"But I wouldn't mind it if we did get married someday."

"This is all so sudden. Why would you—"

"Because you're my best friend. The best woman I've ever known. And the only woman I've ever loved."

She looked at him as she blinked away the tears that had filled her eyes.

"Why wouldn't I want to be with you?"

"Because, Dean, your life has been the complete opposite of settling down. You've never known what it was like to settle down. You might be here for three months and hate it."

He shook his head. "Could never."

"You don't know."

"I do."

"You don't."

"Hey, will you pretend you trust me for a second and think about what our life might be like together?"

Her eyes shut tightly. "Dean, I've thought about that since I was a girl."

A knot formed in his stomach at her confession. When he was younger, he never imagined a life without her. "What's it like?"

She sighed. "We wake up on a Sunday morning and we bicker about who has to get up to put on the coffee."

"Sounds about right," he chuckled and then kissed her hand. "What else?"

"We have a very good baby. Very well-behaved."

"That's wishful thinking."

Mel grinned as she shut her eyes. "It's a girl. And she loves you more than me. A real daddy's girl."

"Impossible."

"And we..." She stopped and opened her eyes. "My childhood fantasy doesn't make sense anymore. Things are so different."

"Nothing will ever be exactly like our fantasy. Sometimes it's better."

She cupped the side of his face and stroked his jaw. "I've got kids, Dean."

"I know. And they're awesome."

"You've talked to them for an hour. They can be demons."

He shrugged. "So were we."

"How can you be so positive about this?"

"Do you need me to say it?"

"I want you to say it," she whispered.

"Because I love you." He kissed her softly. "I love every part of you. Every part of your life. And…" He squeezed her hand. "I want to be a part of it."

Mel laughed. "You're crazy."

"So are you."

"I know. And I love you for it."

Dean sighed, his eyes widening in disbelief. "Really?"

She nodded as she looked at him with a tender gaze. "I love everything about you. I always have."

Dean pressed his forehead to Mel's.

"We can try," she said, "but you have to know that my girls come first."

"I understand."

"They need to love you as much as I do if this is going to work."

He kissed every knuckle on her hand, murmuring, "I'll do whatever I can to make that happen. I promise."

Her eyes flooded with tears. "You really want to have a life with me?"

Dean smiled, but tears were pricking his eyes as well. "I really want to have a life with you."

With that final admission sent into the universe, Mel pushed herself into his arms as close as she could be, kissing him with all her might. Dean embraced her tightly. Every kiss felt better and better knowing that it would not be the last.

Something in his gut told him he'd get to kiss Mel for the rest of his life.

If you enjoyed this book, please consider leaving a review: https://amzn.to/48XBw1A

Turn the Page

Chapter One

Ginny DePowell pointed her flashlight out the passenger window and scanned the side of the road as the police cruiser crept down the dark street.

"Any sign of her?" Officer Melanie Hart asked from behind the steering wheel.

Anxiety tightened Ginny's chest and stole her breath. Before she could answer, rustling in a bush drew her attention. She jerked the light toward the shaking leaves, only to find a spooked raccoon standing in high alert.

"No." Ginny clicked off the light as the scavenger turned and ran. "Damn it, Mom. Where are you?"

Mel put her hand on Ginny's arm and offered a reassuring smile. "We'll find her. We always do."

Ginny nodded. "I'm sorry to drag you away from your dinner break."

"Don't be silly." Mel turned her gaze back to the road. "This is much more important."

Her kindness nearly brought tears to Ginny's eyes. Ever since her mother had started wandering out of the house the year before, Mel was always there to help, regardless of the time of day or what she was doing. Tonight, she must have barely finished heating up her dinner when she'd gotten the call. The smell of her food filled the vehicle from the plastic container that sat between them.

As soon as Ginny had climbed into the car and realized Mel hadn't gotten to eat, she apologized and suggested she finish the meal, but her friend insisted she could wait. While they started their search, Mel recited the recipe for the quinoa and pepper pilaf she'd reheated at the station before getting Ginny's plea for help.

Ginny appreciated the effort to distract her and soothe her nerves, but she had tuned out most of what Mel was saying. If Ginny hadn't gotten up to get a glass of water and noticed the front door open, she wouldn't have realized her mom had wandered off until morning. That terrified her.

The police radio bristled with static, pulling Ginny from her thoughts. Seconds later, Officer Chet Hudson's deep baritone came through. "Hart? You there?"

Mel grabbed the receiver. "You got something, Hudson?"

"Family Time Café. Back booth."

"Heading that way now." Mel hung up and flipped on the red and blue lights that sat atop her vehicle. Though she didn't turn on the siren, she increased her speed. Ginny's mom was in good hands at the café, but Mel wasted no time getting them there. She sped through the streets of the small town of Cloverton, Illinois.

In less than five minutes, they were at Family Time Café, the last remaining twenty-four-hour spot in town. Most of the other businesses gave up catering to the town's dwindling number of shift workers years ago.

"I'll be here when you're ready to go home," Mel called as Ginny climbed from the car.

She spotted Chet in the back row of booths. He and his wife had been friends with Ginny's parents for years. When her father died in a car accident ten years before, Chet and Tanisha had been there, not just for the funeral, but sorting out insurance and helping Ginny and Alice find their way as a family of two.

No matter how lost her mother seemed to become in the fog of her mind, she always recognized Chet.

Her mom sat in the booth with a stack of pancakes in front of her. A man with dark blond hair and wire-rimmed glasses sat next to her. His close-trimmed beard seemed out of place on his youthful face. He appeared to be a few years younger than Ginny and wore a pleasant smile as he cradled a mug between his palms.

The stranger said something, and Alice laughed as if eating pancakes in her pajamas at the local café in the middle of the night was perfectly normal.

"For God's sake," Ginny muttered with frustration. Not at her mother. Alice couldn't help what dementia had done to her. Ginny directed her anger at the invisible foe stealing her mom a little at a time. After taking a calming breath, Ginny faked a smile and headed to the booth.

Chet greeted her warmly. "Good evening."

"Hi, Chet," she said. "I haven't seen Tanisha at the store for a while. How is she doing?"

He nodded slightly at the reference to his wife. She'd been battling breast cancer for the last six months. Some days were better than others, or so they both liked to tell anyone who asked. "The latest round of chemo was hard on her. You should see her soon."

Ginny tilted her head sympathetically. "I'm happy to send over some books if she's too tired to get out."

"I'll let her know that, Ginny. Thank you."

She turned her attention to the woman at the table. "Mom."

"Ginny, I was telling my friends about the time you got locked up in City Hall. Do you remember that? Fall Festival in, oh gosh, '93, maybe? You were..." Her words faded and her eyes glazed over as she tried to recall.

Ginny didn't have the heart to remind her mother it had been Stephanie, Ginny's best friend since preschool, who had sneaked into City Hall on a dare and had inadvertently gotten locked inside. Ginny and Stephanie had been like sisters growing up—they'd always been together. Alice seemed to blur the lines in her memories between the two much more often these days.

Ginny eyed the stranger. "Who's your friend?"

The man's smile warmed even more. "Ben Weaver," he offered with a gentle voice that soothed Ginny's frayed nerves. The kindness in his tone was undeniable.

"He found Alice wandering down Main Street," Chet offered softly. "Brought her here to get her warmed up."

"I would have called the police, but Officer Hudson was here," Ben said finishing the tale.

Alice piped up as well. "Chet ordered me pancakes." Her smile widened. "Jamal let me have pumpkin pancakes even though they aren't on the menu until October."

Rather than point out that October was less than an hour away, Ginny smiled warmly. "Well, he likes you. He always says so." Ginny swallowed hard as the urge to cry hit her. The evening could have turned out differently if the stranger's intentions hadn't been good. Or if he'd ignored a woman wandering in her nightgown during the night.

Thankfully, Alice was now wearing a dark brown too-large sweater rolled at the wrists. Ginny glanced under the table and sighed with relief to see a pair of slippers on her mother's feet. At least she hadn't been wandering around in bare feet. The cooler temperatures of October had set in.

"Is that your sweater?" she asked Ben. When he nodded, she started to remove her jacket, but he held up a hand to stop her.

"I'll get it tomorrow."

"Thank you. I own—"

"In Good Time." He smiled across the table. "Alice told me all about your bookstore."

Despite her stress, Ginny gave him a soft smile. "I appreciate that. I open at ten."

He nodded slightly and then made a show of heaving a big sigh. "It was great chatting with you, Alice, but I need to get home now."

Alice didn't seem to hear him as she focused on her late-night snack. He slid from the booth and disappeared without another word.

"Thanks for looking out for her," Ginny said to Chet.

"Don't mention it." He lifted his mug. "I need a refill."

Ginny peered out the window at Mel's cruiser. In the lights shining through the café window, she watched her friend wipe her hands on a napkin. In the time Ginny had been standing there getting her mind around Alice's latest adventure, Mel finally had a chance to eat her dinner. "Could you tell Mel she can go? No need for her to wait." She focused on Alice slowly cutting her pancakes. "We may be here for a while."

"Yeah, of course. And when you two are ready, I'll drive you home. I'll be over at the counter."

"Thanks, Chet."

He took his cup and slid from the booth. He put his hand on Ginny's shoulder, giving her a comforting squeeze. "Alice, it was good to see you."

"You too, as always." Alice took his other hand in hers. "Thank you." Her eyes had filled with clarity. The haze that had been there before cleared up, at least for the moment.

After Chet left them, Ginny slid into the booth where he'd been sitting.

Alice looked at her sheepishly. "I think I got confused again."

"Yes, seems that way."

Ginny used to think they had so much time left together but every episode that sent her searching for her mother was a reminder that she wouldn't be able to safely care for Alice in their small two-bedroom home for much longer.

"Have some of my pancakes," her mom whispered. "Then we'll go home."

The stress of searching for her during the night slipped away, and Ginny reached for the utensils still rolled in a paper napkin. She had to treasure every pleasant moment with her mother she could. Sharing pumpkin pancakes at eleven p.m. seemed like something she would like to remember someday.

The collar of Ginny's sweater tickled her chin as she let out a long yawn the next afternoon. She readjusted the turtleneck and then skimmed the contents of the box on the counter. "Evie?" she called into the shop.

The young woman popped her head out from an aisle of books. Her long, dark, wavy pigtails bobbed with her. "Yeah?"

Ginny sighed at her eager response, wishing she had half the energy of the willowy high school student who worked at the bookstore part-time.

"Could you make a delivery to Mr. Brown at the paper?" Ginny tucked an invoice between two books. Most of the titles were historical retrospectives and biographies.

"Do you want me to do that before or after I've finished organizing the art books?" She glanced down the aisle.

Ginny closed her eyes and rubbed her temples. "I forgot I asked you to do that."

Evie gestured toward the table set up close to the front door. "And you wanted me to change out the banned books display to spooky stories for Halloween."

"Right." Ginny eyed the table. Customers had whittled the choices down over September, much to her delight.

"And I also—"

"Okay," Ginny interrupted with a half-hearted laugh, "put your tasks on hold and go deliver this." There was too much to do around the store for two people. She dug into her pocket and pulled out a ten-dollar bill. "You can swing by the bakery and grab us a treat on your way back."

Evie's thick-soled canvas shoes clomped as she bounded over and swiped the money from her hand. "Nice." Despite her tendency to dress in dark, baggy clothing, Evie Hilton was bubbly and practically bounced wherever she went.

"But don't get caught up visiting with your sister," Ginny warned. "Come right back."

"Marybeth isn't working today." Evie grabbed the box and turned toward the door.

"Thank you," Ginny called after her.

The bell above the door jangled as Evie left the shop.

Though exhaustion had settled deep into her bones, Ginny abandoned the register to check some things off the to-do list she'd dumped on her helper. At the display table, she gathered a stack of books to return to their proper spots.

Ginny's paternal grandfather had owned the store since the 1950s and, when he'd passed away, Ginny had inherited it. Her father had liked his job at the logging company and her grandpa hadn't wanted it to leave the family. As his only grandchild, Ginny had been the most logical person for him to leave it to. And she loved him even more for it.

Though the store wasn't the booming business it had once been, Ginny couldn't imagine ever letting the doors close.

Located right on Main Street, in the historic district, the storefront was the same gray stone used over a hundred years ago. Inside, the original wooden floors were polished to a shine and beautiful crystal chandeliers cast the entire first floor in a soothing light that maintained the charm of an old-time store. In the back, a spiraling wrought iron staircase decorated like a castle turret led to the children's section.

The store was her home away from home.

She drifted around the aisles until she came to the last book in her stack: *Lady Chatterley's Lover*. Even though she had been scolded by several older patrons for putting the book out, many asking her what her grandfather would think, it had flown off the shelves. As she walked to the classics aisle, she opened the book to a random page and a passage caught her eye—a section about how loneliness only fades in small gaps of time.

She frowned. For a story known for being salacious and romantic, she had stumbled upon one of the saddest passages, so like her loveless circumstances.

"Hi, Ginny."

She jumped, causing the book to fall to the ground with a dull thud as she spun to find a man at the end of the aisle. Not just any man. The man who had walked her mom to the café the night before. Ben Weaver. She remembered because she'd repeatedly played the casual way he'd shared his name in her mind the night before. As soon as her mom was tucked into bed and the house was quiet, Ginny had carried his sweater downstairs. His scent—something spicy—had drifted from the ragg wool and filled her senses. She'd spent far too long thinking of his soft smile and kind voice. Thinking of him had stopped her from thinking about all the horrible things that could have happened if he hadn't walked Alice to the café.

"I'm so sorry," he said with an apologetic smile. "I didn't mean to scare you."

"It's okay. I was in my own world. Occupational hazard." She offered him a light, uneasy laugh as she bent for the book, but Ben scooped it up before she could.

"*Lady Chatterley's Lover?*" His eyes met hers, and she noticed how pristinely gray they were, like storm clouds. A friendly, closed-lipped grin appeared on his lips. "It's a good one."

Her face flushed. "Yes, it's been a while since I've visited it." She took the book from him and slipped it into the proper spot on the shelf.

"Visited," he repeated. "I like that."

"Well, that's what it feels like to reread a good book, doesn't it? It's like going to see old friends and visiting old haunts."

He chuckled. "Yes, it is like that. Although I'm afraid with so many books to read and so little life to live, I find less and less time to revisit."

She gestured aimlessly toward the front of the store. "I didn't hear the bells chime when you came in. I was distracted."

His smile faded. "Is your mom okay?"

She shrugged slightly. "Sure. She's fine today. Like nothing ever happened." She looked down for a moment before mustering her strength with a deep breath.

"I'm sorry," he said. "I didn't mean to upset you."

"You didn't."

"I tend to say the wrong thing at the wrong time." His half-hearted smile returned. "I have a way of sticking my foot in my mouth."

"You didn't say the wrong thing," she assured him. "Mom has problems with her memory. Sometimes she gets it in her head that she's supposed to be somewhere else and wanders off before I realize she's gone. Thank you for taking care of her last night. I really appreciate it."

The warmth that she'd seen in his eyes the night before returned. "She's lovely. I enjoyed chatting with her. *Visiting* with her," he amended.

Ginny hoped he was sincere and not simply placating her. The only thing worse than watching her mother's health deteriorate was the sympathy people bestowed on her.

"How are you?" he asked, surprising her. "You seemed shaken last night."

She debated how to answer his question before saying, "I'm okay. Thank you for asking. Your sweater is up front." Stepping around him, she led him to the counter.

They didn't speak again until she pulled his folded cardigan from where she'd stored it that morning. As she did, she nodded at the copy of *Spoon River Anthology* by Edgar Lee Masters tucked under his arm. "Interesting choice."

He held the book in both hands, admiring the cover. "It's a beautiful copy. If I'm correct, Masters based the poems on a small town in Illinois. Much like this one."

"Yes. Although it's farther west." When he held the book to her, she shook her head. "On the house. A thank-you for looking after my mother."

He hesitated before nodding. "I appreciate that."

"I haven't seen you around. Are you new to town?"

"Yes. I got here yesterday."

She tilted her head. "And you were wandering the streets at eleven in the evening?"

A bashful grin curved his lips. "I couldn't sleep, and it seemed like a good time to learn the lay of the land. I'd been told the café is the best place for insomniacs to visit."

"We used to have several businesses with shift workers. Having a restaurant open at all hours made sense then.

I'm not sure it still does, but old habits in old towns." An awkward giggle left her, and she pressed her lips closed to stop it.

Though the conversation was easy, she felt nervous and unsure of herself. Ben's stare was kind but intense as if he were reading her deepest thoughts and darkest secrets. Not that she had either. Ginny's life had been fairly simple and straightforward. Boring.

She shifted from one foot to the other. "Are you just passing through, then?"

Ben set the book on top of his sweater. "Actually, I'm going to be here for a bit. Maybe a while."

She lifted a brow at him. "That's a cryptic answer."

"Not cryptic as much as undecided."

"Fair enough. Would you like a bag?"

He tucked his items under his arm. "No thanks."

Ginny rested her hands on the counter. "You must be from Chicago."

His big smile revealed long dimples. "How'd you guess that?"

"People from the city always refuse bags." Cloverton was well within driving distance of the city. People from the metropolis and surrounding areas used to flood Cloverton's streets, back before the population had thinned and so many shops had closed. Unfortunately, a series of closings, starting with the logging company that had been the town's lifeblood, had caused tourists to bypass the once bustling little town to go elsewhere.

"I was getting my master's from the University of Chicago."

"Wow. In what?"

"Writing. Fiction, to be specific."

How fitting for his mysterious charm. The man was more intriguing by the minute. A stranger settling in Cloverton for an unclear amount of time. A writer. "What do you write? Besides fiction."

"Slice of life type stuff," he said as a blush touched his cheeks.

She couldn't stop the excitement from filling her chest. "Like *The House on Mango Street*? I love that book."

He nodded. "I guess something along those lines. I hired an editor to help me polish my manuscript, and he thinks the town in my book falls flat. He suggested I spend some time in a town like this to get the feel of it."

Ginny's smile spread. "And so you came here. Just like that?"

He shrugged. "It probably sounds impulsive."

"It sounds amazing. To just... To dive in like that." She couldn't imagine picking up her life and going some-where else. "You've chosen well. Cloverton is a wonderful little town, though we aren't as busy as we used to be. The logging company closed and took quite a bit of our small-town charm with it. I like to think we are bouncing back, though."

Ben shifted and pressed his lips together as if he didn't know how to say what was on his mind. She must have made him uncomfortable. She hadn't intended to. She'd only meant to show him she was interested, then again, maybe that was what had made him uneasy. There was a difference between people from Cloverton and Chicago, even though they were only separated by an hour drive. People from the city didn't like being seen. She'd likely overstepped by commenting on his personal business.

"Listen, you wouldn't happen to need any help around here, would you?" he asked. "I planned on spending the day applying around town, but I'd love to work in a bookstore. If you're hiring."

She lifted her brows. "Hiring?" she asked as if the idea were foreign to her.

"Your mom told me about all the work that needs to be done to run the store. Sounds like a lot and, well, I'm a writer," he said with a casual shrug. "Working here would definitely be within my skillset."

She scanned the store, pausing on the books that still needed to be reshelved so others could be put on display, and thinking of all the other things she had to do. Sure, she had Evie and sometimes her friend Stephanie popped in. When Alice had her wits, she was as good as anyone else. She'd grown up in the store too. But someone who knew about books and authors? She could use one of those. "I can't pay much."

"That's okay. I do a lot of freelance work, which is great, but I need a little extra to help make ends meet. I'll take what I can get."

"It would be part-time," she added.

He grinned. "I'm eyeballs deep in editing my manuscript. Part-time is perfect."

She considered him for a moment. He embodied the bookish grad student perfectly, with his glasses and mused dress shirt unbuttoned just enough to reveal the tender pocket of his collarbone and a gentle spray of chest hair. And he was attractive with high cheekbones, blushing red lips, and those cool but friendly eyes. His close-cut facial hair looked like a five o'clock shadow, adding an air of mystery.

Plus, he was a newcomer to a town that rarely had those. That alone would draw in customers. They would flock to the store to subtly check him out, get a feel for him as if they had the right to approve of his presence.

She took one of the business cards from the holder on the counter and held it out to him. "Email me a resume with a few references."

"Cool," he said with a nod.

"Could you come in tomorrow afternoon? For a quick interview and maybe to help out a bit to see how it goes."

"Perfect." He stared at the card for several long seconds before softly saying. "Ginny DePowell."

A feeling she couldn't describe rolled over her at the sound of her name on his lips. She took a shuddering breath before forcing a smile. "That's me," she said slightly breathless.

He looked up, meeting her eyes, before holding his hand out. "Nice to meet you, Ginny."

She took his hand and admired the way his fingers curled around her palm. "Nice to meet you, Ben."

When their hands separated, she felt an unexpected sense of emptiness. "Tomorrow. Two p.m."

"Sounds good," he said with a charming voice. "I'm already looking forward to it." As he backed away from the counter, he scanned the aisles of books and the metal spiral staircase and then stopped on the chandelier over the entryway. "You've got a beautiful place here."

She beamed. Few people his age, let alone men, would take the time to appreciate the ambiance of the old store. "Thank you. I think so too."

Ben smiled at her with childlike excitement in his eyes. "See you tomorrow." And then, he slipped outside, causing the bells to jangle.

She watched through the big window until he disappeared down the street. Only then did she realize her heart was thumping. Putting her hand to her chest, she let out a slow breath and did her best to dismiss the odd feeling that had settled low in her stomach.

Also By Haven Saunders with Marci Wilson

Cloverton Romance Series

Turn the Page: Book One
Faked With Love: Book Two
Music of the Heart: Book Three
In Full Bloom: Book Four
Tattered Dreams: Book Five
By Design: Book Six (coming soon)

We would love to hear from you!

Haven Saunders:
Website: https://havensaunders.com/
Email: havensaundersauthor@gmail.com

Marci Wilson:
Website: www.marciwilson.com
Email: marciwilsonauthor@gmail.com